Lazelle &
Susanne,

Thank you for your
support & inspiration at the
retreat!

# Love and Mardi Gras

*Laissez Les Bons
Temps Rouler!*

A NOVEL BY

## LAURYN PEÑA

Fulton Books, Inc.
Meadville, PA

Published by Fulton Books 2021

ISBN 978-1-64952-864-3 (paperback)
ISBN 978-1-64952-865-0 (digital)

Printed in the United States of America

There are a lot of places I like, but
I like New Orleans better.
                              —Bob Dylan

For Sara,
In honor of your friendship and encouragement

# Contents

# CHAPTER 1

## *LA*

FLASHING BLUE LIGHT filled the dark room; the sound of sirens broke the silence like an unwelcomed intruder. Lisa jolted, her heart raced, startled by the sudden burst of noise that disrupted the peace and quiet of the early morning hours. Her body shook as she moved slowly to disarm the alarm from her phone that lay on the night stand; 5:00 AM was displayed on the face of her phone. Lisa let out a sigh of relief, the room was quiet, dark, and peaceful again. Her body felt weak and trembled with every move she made. Her eyes felt heavy as she lay flat on her back. She continued to stare at the blank white ceiling, in a trance for what felt like days. As she laid in bed, she desperately wished her mind was as blank as the ceiling, so she could get at least one hour of sleep that night. The silence of an empty room that was once her solace, was now her enemy, like a lot of things she once loved. Insomnia was the most hated companion to the depression she now endured.

She sat on the edge of the bed and mustered the energy to stand. Her ankle cracked as she walked slow and stiff like a mummy. She used the light of her phone to guide her across the dark room. She was making an effort to be as quiet as possible. She spent the night in the guestroom of her friend's apartment, and didn't want her friend to be affected by her insomnia through the paper-thin walls. Lisa opened her travel app to check the status of her flight; *On Time*, was displayed in bold green on the top right corner of her mobile boarding pass. Once her eyes acclimated to the bathroom lights, she started to feel excited to be going on this spontaneous trip that was two days in the making. She was excited to escape California and fly to New Orleans.

She looked at herself in the mirror and was shocked at her reflection. She hardly recognized herself. She grimaced as she examined the dark circles around her eyes. She averaged about three hours of sleep per night if she was lucky. She had recently come to the conclusion that the hour of 4:00 AM to 5:00 AM is the hour when no logical person is intentionally awake. The club crowd usually got home around 3:00 AM, and the joggers usually began their jogs around 5:00 AM. Sometimes, during her insomniac nights, she would reminisce about her happiest moments in her early twenties when she lived on the coast of Spain; 4:00 AM was a time that she would stumble home from a night out. She would sit on the city steps of the plaza and indulge in a late-night crepe with friends. They would recap the shenanigans of the evening before being guided home by the glow of the moon and streetlights that illuminated the white Mediterranean buildings. They would walk along the cobblestone streets, while being held in the comfort of the warm summer night air that made you feel like a kid again. Those nights made 4:00 AM feel like an hour of freedom, a freedom that she desperately missed.

It had been three months since her fiancé dumped her for his coworker. At first, she missed feeling his warm body asleep next to her. She missed the feeling of protection, she missed hearing him breathe, she missed having to lightly nudge him as he snored. She missed the fancy mattress he had bought for them. She missed Sunday mornings when he would get up early to go running, then would return with her favorite latte. She missed his adventurous palate when she wanted to cook a new recipe, or try a new restaurant. But now all she missed was sleep. She recently moved into a new apartment and was trying to transition to sleeping alone in a completely new environment. At least, that is what she told her friends and family when they would comment on her lack of energy, dark circles under her eyes, and loss of weight. *I'm fine* was always her default answer. She wore the mask of confidence well. But she was not fine. She was falling apart.

She had been dumped in the most cowardly way. She'd almost preferred a simple text. Nothing special or poetic, just two words of honesty that simply stated *It's over*. Instead, she received months of lies. Her suspicions were confirmed when she caught them kissing at the Yogurtland near his work. He seemed stressed, so she decided to give him a sweet surprise and bring him frozen yogurt during his lunch hour. Instead, she was the one who was surprised when she walked into the shop and saw them holding hands, kissing. They kissed with familiarity, like they were used to kissing each other, not a new love's kiss. She caught them in a way that he couldn't lie about any longer.

Los Angeles had become a constant reminder of the breakup. Her favorite restaurants didn't taste good anymore, their favorite date night haunts made her grimace. And she avoided the general areas where he worked and lived. Los Angeles is known as the city of miracles, hope, and opportunity. But to Lisa, it was the city of tough love. Her romantic love story had turned into a drama. She was desperate to start over and rewrite the screenplay of her life. Which is why she jumped at the opportunity to take a weekend to forget the failures and escape LA. In a few short hours, she'd be arriving in New Orleans for the Mardi Gras weekend.

Lisa threw on a pair of jeans, a comfy loose-fitting sweater, and tennis shoes. She applied concealer to the dark circles and minimal makeup to the rest of her face. She dabbed water, argan oil, mousse, and spritz of hairspray. She arranged her brown curly hair in a way that did not look like she just rolled out of bed. Lisa had mastered the messy yet put-together look. She walked across the dark hallway to her friend Allison's room and slowly opened the door.

"Allison, wake up, we have to leave in ten minutes," Lisa whispered gently.

"Okay," Allison replied, with her eyes still closed and her body in the same position as she always sleeps.

Originally, Lisa had planned to stay at Allison's house and call a Lyft to take her to LAX, since Allison lives ten minutes from the airport. But Allison insisted on driving Lisa to the airport. Lisa gathered her belongings and waited in the living room like a child waited for the school bus. Allison emerged from her room dressed in gym clothes, and her hair up in a tight bun. They exited the apartment into the narrow fluorescent-lit hallway.

"Did that guy you met at the bar last night text you?" Lisa asked Allison as they walked toward the elevator.

Allison yawned. "Nope, he's probably waiting that three-day buffer or whatever."

"Why do guys think that's an acceptable rule? If you like someone, just send a text, no waiting game," Lisa replied with gusto.

"Exactly! Oh well, I'm just glad to have our wing women duo back! I mean you never stopped being my wing woman. But after all those years, it's fun to be out on the single prowl with you again."

"Yeah, we're both finally single at the same time! We only had those first two years of college with no guys taking up all our time," Lisa responded.

The elevator doors opened as soon as Lisa hit the button. The elevator had clearly not been used since they got back from the bars the previous night. They were the last residents home and the first ones to leave. They took the elevator down to the basement parking lot where Allison's car was parked.

"Do you think you'll meet anyone in New Orleans?" Allison asked as they walked toward the car.

"I don't know, I'll be with my family, so it might be hard. But a weekend fling sounds like a fun idea."

"You definitely deserve one. Your birth chart says you'll have great energy for the next few days! Have you been seeing 5s or 1s repeating?" Allison said as she popped the trunk open for Lisa to put her carry-on into the already crowded trunk of beach blankets, yoga mats, and reusable shopping bags.

As she put her carry-on into the trunk Lisa replied, "I haven't paid attention to any repeating numbers actually."

"Well if you do, let me know," Allison responded in sincerity as they both buckled their seat belts and drove out of the garage.

Lisa always enjoyed early mornings in LA; she always felt like there was a special sense of calm and ethereal presence felt during those hours. Everything was blue, providing the feeling of being inside one of Picasso's paintings. The magic that was felt in the early morning haze covered the poverty on the streets while the darkness provided a camouflage to the facade of wealth and fame. The air was fresh, the wind was calm, the streetlights were transitioning to turn off as the sun rose, giving the streets a golden color to adequately portray the state's nickname: the golden state. The only businesses that were open were gas stations and Starbucks, the main sources of fuel for the two main habitants of Southern California. As the sun rose slowly over the San Bernardino Mountains, and the surfers eased into the waves, the stereotypical laid-back persona of California was found within its own nature.

However, the peace was short lived. As soon as Allison's car exited the freeway into LAX, the Hollywood diva that controls the soul of the city reminded everyone immediately who called the shots. Cars were lined up with people, anxiously trying to make their flights. Adults were reverted to children speeding around the airport like a go-kart racetrack. Drivers were immediately turned into defensive specialists, but a good driver tried their best to make sure they were always in the correct lane. One missed gap could turn a quick five-minute drop off, to a thirty-minute loop around the airport. Allison, an LA native, took her teenage driver's test in these chaotic conditions. She handled the traffic with the accuracy of a Formula One champion. She swiftly merged into the correct lanes and pulled into the departure terminal. They both exited the car in the drop-off lane and quickly walked toward the trunk.

"Thank you so much for taking me to the airport," Lisa said while gathering her things from the trunk of Allison's black sedan.

"Of course, it's my pleasure. Besides, it's good motivation for me get up early enough to go to the gym! Last night was so much fun, we for sure need to go back to that bar when you get back. Have fun and text me when you get there."

She smiled. "I will."

As she hurried toward the terminal entrance. She waved good bye to Allison.

"Love and light," Allison said as she held her hands in the air open toward Lisa. She quickly got back into her car and drove away from the departure terminal.

Lisa positioned her bags and began walking and rolling her carry-on into the already crowded security line. As Lisa stood in line, she began scanning her surroundings. She wondered if she'd recognize anyone. Anyone famous? Any friends? The dreaded ex? She prepared herself for the walk through the body scanners: shoes in one bin, purse in another, scarf, jacket, and belt in another bin. Lisa loaded her items on the conveyor belt then stood on the yellow painted feet markings as she waited to be waved through the scanning machine by the TSA agent. She felt relief when she wasn't flagged and patted down. She didn't have anything to hide; she just hated attention, she thought it was frightening to get pulled aside with everyone looking at her curiously and judgingly.

Lisa walked through the sleepy terminal looking for a place to keep occupied for the next hour before her boarding time. Most of the shops were closed, except Starbucks, which had a line that greatly exceeded her patience threshold. She felt antsy; she wanted a cocktail. Lisa saw a sports bar that was open and quickly walked toward the direction of the orange neon sign. The bar was empty with only one waitress working. Lisa walked to the counter and sat down.

"Good morning, what can I get you?" the waitress asked Lisa.

Without looking at any menus or signs, Lisa said, "Good Morning, I'll take a margarita please."

"Sorry, ma'am, we don't serve alcohol before 7:00 AM."

"Oh, what time is it?"

"6:45 AM," the waitress responded quickly with an unamused look on her face.

"Okay, umm I'll just take a croissant and bottle of water to go then."

Lisa wasn't hungry, but she knew she would get hungry in about two hours when she was on the plane. She asked for something relatively normal for the time and situation, and she wanted to make the waitress believe she wasn't an alcoholic. After a few minutes, the waitress arrived with her order and her check. Lisa paid the bill in cash then promptly left the bar to sit at her terminal to anxiously wait for boarding.

As she sat in the uncomfortable rubber chairs at her gate, Lisa was more fidgety than usual. It was her first trip since the breakup. Just the mere thought of running into the ex made her want to hide in the bathroom stall until her boarding time. She stayed resolute and sat at her gate as she anxiously waited to escape California. Suddenly, a voice caught her attention. "Yes ma'am," he said as he spoke into his phone while walking through the terminal. His voice was southern and polite. She looked up from her phone and saw a man around her age. He was well-dressed and well-mannered, a typical southern gentleman. *I need to find a guy like that!* Lisa thought to herself. As much as she wanted to talk to this southern catch, she kept to herself.

Lisa missed being in a relationship. She tended to fall quickly for guys and get swept up in the romance. She was fearless when it came to dating. However, her tendency to become so swept up in her relationships caused her to lose a sense of her own identity. She had spent most of her twenties thinking in a *we* mentality, that she did not know what it was like to think about *me*. Relationships made her feel validated. She felt like she had a purpose when she had someone else to take care of. She felt like part of her was missing, and longed to find the missing piece. She hoped that missing piece would be found in New Orleans.

# CHAPTER 2

## *NOLA*

LISA OBSERVED HER fellow travelers as they anxiously awaited to jump out of their seats like a jack in the box. As soon as the captain turned off the seatbelt sign, passengers clogged up the walkway. They rushed to get off the plane, escaping their cabin fever.

Lisa had been feeling that way about life in general. She wanted to get away, clear her head, and start fresh some place new. She wanted to enter this new season of her life with a bang. As the rows in front of her economy class seat started to gather their carry-ons from the overhead bins, she texted Allison, and her parents, to let them know she landed safely in New Orleans.

As she walked out of the Jetway, she was greeted by green, purple, and gold streamers, bows; Mardi Gras decorations were everywhere.

"Whoa," she said as she took in the decorations.

*Am I still in America?* Lisa thought as she walked through the airport that was festively decorated. The air was filled with excitement and suspense. There was the pageantry of Christmas but the camp of Halloween. Upon entry into the city, Mardi Gras is celebrated like a national holiday, though it only happens in New Orleans.

"Excuse me, sir?" Lisa asked a man who worked at the airport.

"Yes, ma'am."

"How do I get to the baggage claim?"

"You keep walking straight in that direction until you see a number four. That is the baggage claim area," the gentleman said while pointing down a long hallway lined with banners and colorful streamers. The hallway was illuminated by electronic promotional posters educating visitors about the great sights to see in New Orleans, famous restaurants, and shopping spots.

"Thank you, sir," Lisa said as she smiled and nodded then walked in the direction pointed to her.

"Happy Mardi Gras!" the gentleman cheerily responded.

*Happy Mardi Gras? Is that a thing people say to each other?* Lisa thought, still wondering if she had left the country. Lisa walked down the hallway, pushing her carry-on, with her shoulder bag secured atop it, looking at the glowing signs as if she were window shopping. As soon as she got to the baggage claim, she saw her aunt, uncle, and younger cousin. Lisa coordinated her flight to arrive at the same time as her family. Her aunt Joan and uncle John lived in New Orleans for years while doing a tour for the Coast Guard. They loved it so much they come back every chance they get. Lisa grew up hearing her family's stories and knew it was a magical time. She had always known that there was something unique and special about this city, which made her even more eager to visit New Orleans.

"Hey, home chicken!" John hollered as Lisa walked toward them.

"Lisa!" her younger cousin, Gabby, yelled.

"Hey, there, girlie!" Joan said as she moved closer to give Lisa a hug.

Lisa's family greeted her with hugs and friendly names that only family could greet one with. "Hey, guys, I'm so excited! I'm finally here!" Lisa responded, happy to see her family. Joan was always a role model of hers. Lisa loved her family very much, and they loved her too.

"Here are your starter beads," Joan said as she put a string of gold, purple, and green beads around her neck. A green and purple mask dangled from it like a medal. Joan put the beads on her as an act of hospitality. It reminded Lisa of her trip to Hawaii and being greeted with a lei.

"Mine has a flower on it!" Lisa's younger cousin, Gabby, exclaimed.

Gabby took after her father as the extroverted life of the party that was curious about everything and everyone. Newly seventeen and close to graduating high school, she'd already been in trouble with boys, booze, and parties.

"All right let's hop on the hotel shuttle," John said.

"We're so excited to share Mardi Gras with you, home slice. Too bad your dad couldn't make it."

"Yeah, oh well, more fun for us, and we can make him jealous, right?" Lisa responded as they walked out of the airport into the noisy tunnel of the loading and unloading zone of car engines and car horns. There was a slight chill in the air. Lisa was glad that she had on her scarf already and didn't bother to pack it in her carry-on. She was surprised at the biting chill she felt on her face. The temperature was not much cooler than Los Angeles, but it felt a lot cooler because of the moisture in the swamp air.

"Here's our shuttle," John said as he quickly grabbed his and Joan's bags.

The driver shook John's hand and helped load the luggage in the back. They all climbed into the shuttle. John sat shotgun, Joan and Gabby sat in the first row, Lisa sat in the last row.

"Did you let your parents know you're here safe?" Joan asked Lisa.

"Yep, I did it while I was waiting to get off the plane."

"Good girl. So, how long has it been since we saw you last? A year maybe? Since your grandparents' fiftieth anniversary party, right?" Joan asked while sitting sideways in the van to face her.

"Yep, that's how long it's been, it's been far too long. How's North Carolina?"

"Well, let me put it this way, you're going to see a lot of rednecks this weekend, and it still won't be as many as the number that live in our town."

"Yeah, we just need to remind ourselves that it's only a four-year tour. It's almost been a year since we moved there, so about thirty-eights months to go," John replied.

It was late in the afternoon, early dusk. The city lights were starting to turn on, one after another. Traffic was starting to line up along the expressway as everyone was trying to get in or out of the city. Lisa and her family had arrived just before the streets started to close for the Friday night parade.

"Hey, look, the super dome is lit up in Mardi Gras colors!" Gabby said while pointing to the Mercedes Benz Superdome.

Lisa marveled at the green, purple, and gold lights illuminating the skyscrapers of the city as they drove closer.

"Wow, they sure go all out for Mardi Gras here, huh?"

John turned his head to look at Lisa and responded in earnest, "You ain't seen nothin' yet, darlin'."

# CHAPTER 3

## *The Roosevelt*

THE VAN QUICKLY pulled up to the hotel. Lisa could tell that the driver was in a hurry to get her family out of the van before the road closures. Lisa got out of the van and looked up in wonder at the art deco signage that was proudly displayed in the front of the hotel; *The Roosevelt, A Waldorf Astoria Hotel* was already lit up and dominated the street. The exterior of the hotel looked like a palace with light gray stone, gold trimmings, and flag poles. Light poured out of the chiseled windows, making the entire building shine like jewels. A short-carpeted staircase led the way to the lobby, which was inlet from the street like a cave. Light from a massive chandelier that hung in the foyer poured out of the entrance, making the hotel feel warm and inviting.

Two doormen walked from their posts to immediately assist them. The driver popped open the back of the van to unload the luggage onto the luggage cart.

Excitedly, John pronounced, "All right, everyone, out, let's get checked in quickly! We don't want to miss Muses!" He was giddy, like a kid who had just arrived at the gates of Disneyland. He was smiling, greeting, and tipping everyone that helped them with their luggage. Lisa looked around at the hotel she was staying at with her family; she smiled as she took in the elegance. She was impressed at the grandeur but nonetheless surprised. Her aunt and uncle tended to stay at five-star hotels. Lisa was a bit of a history nerd, and she could tell that The Roosevelt Hotel was filled with history by just looking at the glowing gilded aged building.

"What's Muses?" Lisa asked Joan as they walked toward the doors of the hotel.

"Muses is the parade that happens tonight, hopefully we won't miss much of it."

"It's thrown by all women," Gabby said.

The hotel was festive with Mardi Gras decorations everywhere. There was a row of chandeliers that lined the long marble hallway of the lobby; they sparkled radiantly like stars in the sky. Lisa fawned over the beautiful flower arrangements that adorned sideboards that lined the halls. The hotel felt magical and opulent like a royal wedding. Everyone was excited and rushing around. As she looked around the lobby, Lisa was intrigued by the vast variety of people. There were the frat boys wearing jeans and ball caps, holding beers, and wearing their beads. Sorority girls in their matching outfits, wearing strings of beads. Men and women of all ages and races walked around in tuxedos and ball gowns with their masks on. People dressed in colorful wigs and crazy outfits. People wore casual clothes with stings of beads. Whatever one wanted to wear, they had license to wear it during Mardi Gras. Families, young and old, were on their way to their specific locations to watch the parade. Once John finished checking in at the front desk, they squeezed into the elevator with their luggage cart and a hotel attendant to guide them to their room.

"What room, Dad?" Gabby asked while taking the key from his hand.

"Room 921," John said while looking at his phone.

"Did you download the parade tracker yet, love?" Joan asked.

"Downloading it now, babe," John responded while still looking down at his phone. The elevator pinged to signal the floor stop. Gabby burst out of the elevator in the direction of the room.

Everything about the hotel was glamourous. Lisa felt like she was transported back to the 1920s. Antique phones sat atop art-deco-inspired tables that looked like they had not been moved since the phone lines were installed; the art deco lettering signage also harkened the time as well. The lights in the hallway were dim and provided the same ambiance as candles, and it smelled like there was a hint of citrus in the air, which had aromatherapeutic elements which made Lisa feel calm. As they all entered the room, Gabby was relaxing on one of the beds, clicking through the channels on the television to see if anything interesting was on.

The hotel attendant followed Lisa and her family, pushing the luggage cart into the room. "Where shall I put the bags, sir?"

"The corner is fine," John responded as he took off his jacket and tossed it on the empty bed.

Lisa and Joan also removed their jackets and sat on the beds, laying down to give their bodies a few minutes of rest before a night of parades.

"Is there anything else I can do for you, Mr. Perez?"

"Nope, I think we're good," John said as he stood up to hand the attendant a tip before he exited the room with the luggage cart. "Okay, y'all, we'll be leaving here in ten minutes," John announced before walking into the bathroom.

"Thanks again for letting me crash your trip and stay here with you. This place is amazing!" Lisa said while looking around the room. She walked over to the window, curious of what sort of view the room had. The view was of the street, overlooking the Orpheum Theater.

"Of course!" Joan replied, "there's no way we'd let you come to New Orleans and not experience the best of it. Wait 'til Sunday, I made reservations at one of my favorite restaurants for brunch, you're going to love it. It's a New Orleans icon and very historical building."

"Awesome, I can't wait!" Lisa replied.

The ladies freshened up, they touched up their hair and makeup. "What should I wear tonight? Are you changing? There were so many people dressed up," Lisa asked Joan.

"I'm wearing this." Joan motioned to the clothes she had on. "If you want to change, you can, but I'm going casual tonight. We're keeping the costumes for tomorrow."

"Okay, good because I don't feel like changing," Lisa responded while smoothing her curly hair with argan oil.

"All right, let's go!" John said while exiting the bathroom.

"What? It hasn't even been ten minutes yet," Gabby said as she put blush on the cheeks of her naturally bronze skin.

"Gosh, you, women, take forever," John complained while plopping into a chair and changing the channels of the television in search of ESPN. The women continued to freshen up and get ready for the night ahead.

Exactly five minutes later, John exclaimed "All right, let's go!" while he turned off the TV and walked toward the door. He was on his way to watch the parade with or without them. The ladies followed hastily. They looked refreshed and proudly wore their starter beads. They quickly boarded the elevator and made their way down. The lobby was still crowded and buzzed with people hurrying in every direction. They walked out of the hotel entrance doors whence they came and onto the winter streets of New Orleans. Lisa buttoned up her coat to combat the cold February air, but she quickly found herself breaking a light sweat as she walked quickly to keep pace with her family. Lisa noticed that the closer they got to the parade route, the more the diversity of cultures, ages, and costumes multiplied. Lisa and her family walked a short distance to Canal Street to wait with the other revelers for the Muses parade to arrive.

# CHAPTER 4

## *Muses*

LISA FELT LIKE she had stumbled into a large party. Thousands of revelers were outside walking around the city, with their starter beads proudly displayed around their necks. The mood was joyous, everyone waited patiently as they lined the sidewalks of Canal Street. Lisa stared at the skyscrapers, streetcar tracks, and palm trees that looked like it lined Canal Street for miles. The tracks and palm trees acted like a border between the old New Orleans and the new New Orleans, the Central Business District and the French Quarter.

As Lisa and her family stood along the parade route, Joan leaned over to Lisa and said, "This is called Canal Street because they had originally planned to build a canal here to make it like Amsterdam. It never got built, but the name stuck."

Lisa was intrigued at this new information. She loved learning the small details of every city she went to visit. She looked down the length of Canal Street in an attempt to try to picture how a canal would look in the city. Clearly it would not be any sort of place suitable for a boat parade, and certainly, it could not hold the thousands of revelers lining it.

"Good lord, I can't imagine how it would've worked out with a canal coming through here with the gators," Gabby commented.

"Ha! Yeah, I never thought about that, Gabs. Because when I was in college at Florida, we'd see them sun bathing on the banks of the pond. So, I imagine they'd do the same on the banks of the canals here," Joan replied.

"Seriously?" Lisa asked in shock that the gators walked around so easily. "I hate gators, they freak me out. They're dinosaurs, like dinosaurs are still here walking around. It's crazy to me."

"Yeah, they're interesting creatures. They're super territorial too. When I was in Miami, one kept coming back to his spot on my flight line. We'd call no-kill catchers to come and take them away, but this one just kept coming back. After a while, they had to put it down because it started to get ornery."

"Yuck," Lisa said as she slightly shook her head and body out of fear and disgust.

"Oh, that's a good spot," John said as he walked in the direction of what he deemed a prime parade viewing location, about 10 feet from where they were originally standing. John led the way while Joan, Gabby, and Lisa followed John's lead.

"Okay this is a good spot," he said while surveying the area, satisfied with his territorial claim. "I'm getting me a daiquiri. Do y'all want one as well?"

"I do," Gabby quickly responded.

"Meant the twenty-one and older folks. I'll get you a soda."

"Yes, please," Lisa replied enthusiastically.

"Yeah, I'll take one too, love," Joan said.

While they waited for their drinks as well as patiently waited for the parade to roll onto Canal Street, a group of people walked by them wearing formal attire. The men wore tuxedos with top hats while the women wore ball gowns. One woman's outfit made Lisa stop and stare. The woman was wearing a long, fitted, white-beaded gown. The white was a perfect contrast to her dark African American skin. She wore white gloves, accessorized with a white feather boa, and diamond jewelry fit for a queen. Her hair was up in a beautiful coiffure that Marie Antoinette might have worn. Her look was topped off with a sparkling gold-and-white masquerade mask with white feathers sticking up from the left side. She was glowing, like the top of a trophy. The feathers, gold beads, sparkling glitter, and rhinestones in the mask made her look angelic.

"Wow, where are they going?" Lisa asked Joan.

"Most of the hotels and clubs here have masquerade balls during the Mardi Gras season. They're most likely going to one of those. We have tickets to one tomorrow night. I told you to bring a long formal dress. Did you remember to bring one?"

"Yeah, I brought a black floor-length bridesmaid dress. But nothing nearly as extravagant as that," Lisa said, discreetly pointing to the woman in white.

"Oh, darling, you're fine, a floor-length dress, beads, and mask is all you need."

"Where can I get a mask?"

"Well, if you don't get one thrown to you tonight during Muses, then we can buy one tomorrow. You can get a mask anywhere here and for pretty cheap too."

"Here are your drinks, ladies, and a coke for you, hun," John said as he handed out the drinks. "I grabbed us some food too," John said as he handed Lisa and the rest of the ladies a bag-filled with corn dogs.

"Thanks, Uncle Johnny," Lisa said as she took a bite into her dog. She had not eaten since her quick layover in Houston and was starting to get hungry. "There's a lot of kids out here tonight. I didn't know kids watch the parades too."

"Mardi Gras is family friendly. The crazy debauchery portrayed in the media and pop culture is mainly only seen on Bourbon Street. But you don't really want to go there right now anyway. There are way too many tourists acting a fool right now. Follow your cousin's lead and secure your real estate," John said while motioning to Gabby who was leaning on the fence lining Canal Street waiting for the parade to begin. Lisa walked over and posted up next to Gabby, who was looking down at her phone texting.

"So, you broke up with Matt?" Gabby asked, not even looking away from her phone.

"Yep. We broke up in the fall."

"That's good. He was cute but weird. He was too quiet and too short for you."

Lisa chuckled at Gabby's response. She liked to hear that her cousin who had only met him once was not impressed by her philandering ex-fiancé.

"Hey! There's the power truck," John said as he made his way to stand next to Lisa and Gabby. "It checks the power lines, and if they are messed up or broken in any way, they repair them so that all the floats can glide beneath safely. It's the first indication that the parade will be arriving very shortly. Following that will be police motorcycles then the parade tracking app car. Then the first krewe, the flambeaux, they're cool, you'll see," John explained to Lisa, already a little inebriated.

Lisa's attention turned down the street where she heard the sounds of motorcycle engines, the NOPD motorcycle cops rode down the street with lights flashing as they made sure the route was safe and orderly. A line of fifteen men carrying what appeared to be propane tanks attached to what appeared to be snow shovels on fire came marching down the street, stopping occasionally to pick stuff up from the ground.

"Who are they?" Lisa asked John.

"Those are flambeaux. In the old days when all the streetlights were gas lamps, guys called flambeaux would walk with lamps to light the way for the parade. New Orleans is a proud city of tradition. It's a very important and historical job, and it's all volunteer, so if you throw money, like change, they pick it up, like this, see?" John proceeded to throw a couple quarters in the street and a flambeaux picked it up.

"I can hear the sirens and music now y'all, wooo-eeee!" John shouted before taking another drink of his daiquiri.

Clicks of a drum line started to get louder and louder as the first marching band approached. Lisa's ears perked up when she heard flutes and other woodwind instruments starting to play the Beyoncé song, "Run the World (Girls)." Lisa and Gabby started to dance along as well as other revelers. Following the marching band closely was the first float, a pink-and-purple high-heeled pump sparkling with glitter and LED lights rolled slowly passed them. A sign that read, *Sing in me Muse and through me tell a story,* was written in perfect calligraphy along the height of the heel. A woman stood at the base of the heel wearing a pink ball gown, a massive campy crown fit for a beauty queen, and threw beads at the revelers. She was the queen of Muses, kicking off the parade. The parade continued with trucks and floats, and people dressed up per the specific theme of their float. Every rider threw beads and Muses paraphernalia.

"This is the first all-female super krewe. That means they have over 1,000 riders. They're a pretty popular and prominent organization in the city, they do a lot of volunteer and philanthropy work," Joan explained to Lisa.

Lisa was happy to hear the information about Muses. She always enjoyed volunteer work and made a mental note to try to find a similar organization to join in California.

School marching bands provided the soundtrack to the night. A high school marching band approached where Lisa was standing. First the color guard walked by with their batons. The band uniforms for this school were red and gold. The drums beat slowly as they marched, Lisa could hear the feet of nearly seventy-five students as they continued to march down Canal Street. The drum major blew his whistle, and the band began playing a lively, upbeat song. Lisa did not recognize the song. *It must be their fight song,* Lisa thought. The trumpets roared and sparkled in the light of the night. The sousaphones shined bright and had a cover on the bell which had an emblem of the school on it. It was dark out, but all the instruments combined with the gold from their uniforms, and large white feathers in their hats, lit up the street. The energy was high, and people were excited. The band marched on. A line of three more parade floats followed closely. One float was designed in a way of mocking the reality show, *The Bachelor.* The float was covered with paper roses, and a large comic strip of women crying, and vying for a man in a tuxedo. The float had women dressed in red and black tutus throwing beads, fake roses, and wearing red masks.

A lively marching band of a local college arrived playing the classic, "Apache (Jump on It)." The band was not in prestige formation; they were all dancing while playing their instruments along with the hundreds of revelers. Everyone yelled "Jump on it" and sang along. Lisa felt like she was in a pep rally again before a big football game. She jumped and sang along with Gabby, Joan, and John.

The next float was in the shape of a giant tube of lipstick and was a bit phallic. Revelers laughed and pointed at it. Next, followed a large purple float. The float was covered in butterflies that sparkled with LED lights. A sign along the side of the float read, *Muses est. 2001*. The riders threw beads, stuffed animals, and plastic shoes to the lucky ones. The decorated, highly coveted shoe was the main throw of the parade. Lisa caught a string of blue beads with a small high heeled glittery pump hanging from it. She was tipsy, and her body was warm from the strong daiquiri. Lisa was enjoying the parade. She was having fun catching beads and indulging in the sights and sounds of the massive street party.

"I'm loving the shoe theme!" Lisa, a shoe lover, said in an excited tone to Joan. She has a healthy preference for fancy footwear and has a large collection in her closet.

Lisa's ears perked up as she heard the yodel of the classic Dolly Parton song, "Mule Skinner Blues". Two mule-drawn carriages were the next floats to pass by their area blaring the classic song with riders dressed as Dolly Parton. Lisa, Joan, and Gabby sang along.

"I love Dolly!" Lisa exclaimed as she half drunkenly tried to sing the lyrics, but it was mainly just a high-pitched yell.

The parade rolled on and on for the next hour with a steady stream of floats, horses, and marching bands. It was one of the liveliest things Lisa had ever experienced. She felt a deep sense of connection to the krewe of Muses. She felt taken under the wing of her aunt, a strong woman that she admired. She also felt an affinity for the parade riders, a group of strong women that established a Mardi Gras krewe and did volunteer service throughout the city. The whole night made Lisa feel inspired. The night provided plenty of role models for her to aspire to be. The parade felt like a grand party, and it was only halfway through. When Lisa first arrived in New Orleans, she did not quite understand the appeal or frenzy of catching beads, but very quickly she fell under the spell of Mardi Gras and began reaching and snatching for beads like a local.

"The big parade happens tomorrow night with Endymion," John said.

This surprised Lisa, she had never experienced such a grand parade before, and Muses was considered small compared to the Endymion parade. The firetruck turned the corner, signaling the end of the parade with the lights shining. It was a beautiful end to a lively parade. Cleanup crews immediately followed with precision and organization to pick up the trash and beads that lined the streets as far as the eye could see. It was midnight. Since Lisa was wide awake with the west coast time of 10:00 PM, she felt exhilarated. She had energy and was excited to be out of the house and enjoying life for the first time in months. She wanted to have new experiences, and luckily, this first night of parades was already helping her achieve her goal of moving on.

"All right, y'all where should we go next?" John asked the ladies.

"How about Café Du Monde? It shouldn't be too crowded right now, and we have to make sure that Lisa experiences that," Joan suggested.

"Sounds good, onward to Café Du Monde," John exclaimed.

# CHAPTER 5

## *Café Du Monde*

THE FRENCH QUARTER was busy and vibrant as revelers dispersed throughout the city in every direction like a spilled drink. The parade was just the pre-game for the hours of partying to resume in every bar and club in the city. Lisa felt like she was in Disneyland, but there were hardly any kids around. Lights, people, and beads were everywhere her eyes could see. Beads hung on every pole and post along the parade route. The closer they got to Bourbon Street, the drunker people were. Lisa was mesmerized by the architecture and European street design while they walked along Decatur Street. She was so enthralled that she didn't notice what was ahead of her. A giant white cathedral glowed in the night and met Lisa with a pleasant surprise.

"Wow!" Lisa said as she stared at the massive St. Louis Cathedral in the heart of the French Quarter.

Lisa and her family were on the river side of Decatur Street. There were stairs that lead to an observation landing. It was a perfect place to take pictures, right along the bank of the Mississippi. The landing had a giant cannon pointed out to the river and a large statue of Andrew Jackson riding his horse, giving the impression that the cannon and Jackson were protecting the city. The white cathedral glowed in the light that shined on it, making it look as if it was a painted backdrop. The cathedral rested perfectly between the French style buildings of the French Quarter. It was perfectly illuminated by the gas lamps surrounding the perimeter of the square. Lisa felt like she had been taken to a place in the past as she stared at this massive building. Lisa and her family stood and looked at the cathedral for a few minutes. Lisa felt gently held in the mystic beauty that seemed primordial. She smiled as she looked at her family, she was happy to be sharing this moment with them.

"I went to a few weddings there when I lived here. It's just as beautiful inside," Joan said to Lisa, standing next to her.

*Ugh, wedding,* Lisa thought. *This would've been a great place for our wedding.* She was still unable to separate her new experiences from her ex. Lisa and her ex had decided to marry at a standard golf course that her ex-fiancé's mother had insisted. Lisa considered herself lucky that his mother had paid the nonrefundable deposit and not Lisa.

"Yep, if New Orleans was originally designed to be the Paris of the Americas, St. Louis would have to be the Eiffel Tower," John commented.

It was indeed beautiful and hard to miss. It dominates the view like the Eiffel Tower. The blue and white lights were soothing to Lisa. The city was busy with revelers and drunks, but this one area stood resolute and remained calm and peaceful.

"Café Du Monde is just right over there, let's keep walking," John said as he pointed to a small building on the corner, about 50 yards from the landing they were standing on. Lisa could see a small building with a green-and-white striped roof and walked toward it, following her uncle.

They grabbed a table just in time to beat the rush of other hungry revelers. Even though the weather was a bit cold and the restaurant was an indoor/outdoor layout, Lisa was not cold anymore. She had a very thick drunk coat on from the booze, and the walking helped keep her blood warm. There was a simple wooden sign that read, *The Original French Market Coffee Stand est. 1862.* The green-and-white stripes were the main decor. The decor gave patrons a feeling of dining in a 1950s restaurant. The tables had white tops to give the impression of cleanliness, which allowed the powdered sugar to blend in. The employee uniforms were also styled in a vintage 1950s type flair that reminded Lisa of In-N-Out burger, a California treasure.

"Welcome, what can I get you?" the waiter said as he approached the table.

"Let's get eight beignets, and I'll take a hot cocoa," John said, motioning to himself. "What do you, ladies, want?"

"Hot cocoa for me, please," Gabby said.

Lisa smiled, "Me, too, please."

"I'll take some chicory coffee please," Joan said.

"Great, it'll be right out," the waiter said with a smile before he turned and walked in the direction of the kitchen.

"So, this is the famous Café Du Monde," Lisa said as she scanned the crowded restaurant. The air smelled sweet like a candy shop. The heaters caused the unlimited supply of powdered sugar to waft throughout the restaurant. It was enough temptation to make even the savory of taste buds crave sugar.

"This place is a treasure. You can't come to New Orleans without eating a beignet," Gabby commented.

"The best time to come is at night. Otherwise, there is a line down the block, and you don't even get to enjoy the atmosphere as much," John said.

"Here is your coffee and cocoa. Your beignets will be out shortly," the waiter said while putting the drinks carefully on the table.

"Good ole Louisiana chicory coffee," Joan said while pouring creamer into her cup, smelling her cup, savoring the smell and slowly taking a sip like a wine connoisseur.

"What's chicory coffee?" Lisa asked.

"It's a type of root that was used to make the coffee during the depression, and people here actually liked it. It remained popular here and pretty much disappeared everywhere else. It has a bit of a spicy kick to it. Do you want to give it a try?" Joan said, motioning to Lisa, holding her cup out to share.

Lisa was hesitant but was reminded of why she came to New Orleans, she wanted to have new experiences. "Sure," Lisa said while reaching for Joan's mug. She took a sip. The spicy bite coated her throat, making her cough and grimace. "Umm, I'll stick with my hot chocolate," she said while sliding Joan's mug back to her side of the table.

"Yeah, chicory coffee is a little too much for me, so I stick with the cocoa when I come here or regular coffee. But that will keep me up all night if I drink it now," John said before taking a drink of his hot chocolate.

"I'm the type that when I travel, I like to do as many local things as possible. I didn't have Starbucks once when I was living in Spain. Some of the other Americans I'd met while traveling still maintained their Starbucks habit, but not me, I refused. But I don't think I can handle a whole cup of that spice," Lisa said.

"That's good, I'm the same way, too, when in Rome, ya know," Joan said before taking another drink of her coffee.

"Here are your beignets," the waiter said while gently distributing the plates of beignets.

John nodded to the waiter and said, "Thank you, sir." As he put a napkin on his lap, he said to the girls, "All right, y'all dig in."

The powdered sugar sat perfectly on the pillows of fried dough like fresh fallen snow on a house. Lisa felt intoxicated by the sweet smell of sugar that permeated from the heat of the beignet. Lisa observed her family to see how they ate beignets. She'd never eaten one before. She didn't know the etiquette for how to eat them without being covered in powdered sugar. They grabbed one each with their hands, then started to bite into the white pillows. Powdered sugar quickly started getting everywhere, even though they ate carefully. Lisa mimicked her family, picking up the beignet, careful not to inhale or breathe through her nose and sneeze the thick layer of powdered sugar all over the table and her family. The powdered sugar touched her lips like a soft fluffy cloud. The sweetness of the powdered sugar filled her mouth, then quickly dissolved. The warmth of the beignet made the rest of her body warm. The crunch of dough added a nice surprise since the dough itself was light and fluffy. It was messy, it was unhealthy, and it was delicious. After they had finished their beignets and drinks, Lisa and her family just sat at the table and mustered up enough energy to walk back to their hotel.

"Since it's late, we should cut through Bourbon Street to get back to the hotel, instead of taking the long way and walking around it," John said as they walked out of the restaurant.

Lisa was a bit nervous to be going to Bourbon Street after what her uncle had initially told her about the drunken debauchery. But she knew he would never put his family in a dangerous position, so she tied her scarf around her neck and followed without fear. She was tired, but her taste buds were satisfied. Lisa thought about the past few months and had realized that was the first meal she had enjoyed since before her breakup. Life was beginning to be sweet again.

They walked down St. Ann Street past St. Louis Cathedral toward Bourbon Street. It was nearly 2:00 AM. The streets were crowded with people drinking, laughing, and congregating. They turned a corner and were greeted by a wall of people and lights: Bourbon Street.

John paused and turned to Lisa and Gabby and said, "Okay, hold on to each other. We're going to walk just down a couple blocks, and we'll be on Canal near our hotel. Gabs and Lisa, if you get lost, just go to a cop, they'll help escort you back to the hotel. Gabby, you don't get rude with these cops, you say 'yes, sir' and 'no, sir.' Do not test these cops, or you will be thrown in jail. This place gets crazy, and you, girls, are too pretty to get lost here." He instructed the women like a general about to lead his troops to battle.

Joan put Gabby in between her and John. They linked arms; Lisa linked arms with Joan. They headed into the crowd. It was warm and smelled of sweat, beer, and everything else that comes out of a person's body when they drink too much. It was surprisingly well lit, with floodlights everywhere and cops standing guard trying to make sure the craziness was confined to Bourbon Street. It didn't feel dangerous, but it would be foolish to test any theories of safety, especially with the NOPD ready for anything. Lisa didn't know where to look. If she looked forward, she might catch the unwanted eye of a drunkard. If she looked down, she lost sight of who was in front of her. If she looked up, she risked being hit in the face by flying beads from the balconies of bars and apartments above. Lisa didn't see any nudity, but since John said the nudity was confined to Bourbon Street, she could only assume that the beads were going to the biggest bidder.

Lisa felt like Dante making his way through one if the circles of hell. As she walked through the crowd, she tripped over beads and go-cups. She felt like she was in a crowded club trying to make her way through the dance floor. They continued onward. John muscled his way through like a professional. He'd lived his twenties in New Orleans, so he was a professional at navigating Bourbon Street. Lisa kept her head down and blindly followed Joan. Just when she thought they would never escape the sea of people, the crowd started to get lighter and lighter, indicating to Lisa that they were near the end. Once they got to the end of Bourbon Street, they unlinked arms to walk around a street barricade that was set up to stop cars from driving onto the street. Two cops were posted near the barricades like guards.

John looked at the cops, nodded, smiled, and said, "Evening sir."

"Having a good night?" one of the cops asked.

"Yes, it's been a fun night," Joan replied. "Time for bed now, good night."

"Have a good night," the other cop replied as he nodded and smiled at John and the ladies like Disneyland cast members escorting riders off a rollercoaster.

Lisa, Gabby, and Joan all nodded and smiled at the cops. The first thing Lisa did when they arrived onto Canal Street was take a giant yoga breath of air. She held her breath for most of the walk because of the smell. *Almost there,* she thought, as she spotted the giant Roosevelt sign illuminating the street. They crossed the mostly empty, and surprisingly clean, Canal Street.

"Good evening, Mr. Perez," the doorman said as he opened the door for Lisa and her family.

"Good evening, sir," John said as they entered the hotel.

The lobby was still bustling with people drinking in the Sazerac bar. The family all showed their bright purple wristbands to the elevator guard who was checking to make sure that only guests of the hotel were accessing the elevators. The guard nodded and gave them access to the elevators. In what felt like an instant, Lisa was in her pajamas with her face washed, teeth brushed, and tucked into the giant bed she shared with Gabby. Everyone was tired, not a whole lot was said as they all rotated through their turns for the bathroom and quickly went to sleep. As Lisa laid in bed, she pondered the events of the past twenty-four hours and how drastically different New Orleans was to Los Angeles. She thought about Muses. Lisa admired the women who started the krewe, and how in a short time, they became a respected super krewe. She couldn't believe the showmanship of the parade and the large amounts of beads that she caught between the talented marching bands and moving works of art that were the parade floats. She could not wait to see what surprises and experiences she would have the rest of the weekend. For the first time in months, she was excited to wake up to a new day.

# CHAPTER 6

## *Sleepless in NOLA*

LISA WOKE UP with a jolt. The shake of her body made the entire bed move. Her heart raced; she looked over to Gabby and was relieved she didn't wake her up. Lisa had the same recurring dream that had been haunting her for months. It always started the same way, she was running along the top of the cliffs of her favorite beach, Corona Del Mar. In her dream, she was the only one running along the trail, but then out of nowhere, her ex starts to run beside her. She immediately turns direction, sprints toward the edge of the cliff, then jumps. She always wakes up just as her feet leave the edge of the rocks. Lisa hoped and prayed every night before falling asleep to not dream about him. But so far, those prayers had gone unanswered, including that night in New Orleans.

Lisa quietly got out of bed; she did not want to awaken or disturb her cousin sleeping next to her. Gabby was clearly not used to sharing a bed with anyone since she took over most of the bed. Lisa was still not used to sleeping alone and stayed on her side of the bed. She looked at her phone to check the time, 6:00 AM in New Orleans, which meant that it was 4:00 AM in Los Angeles. *Of course*, she thought. Like clockwork, she was up at 4:00 AM. Using the glow of her phone to light the way to the bathroom, she maneuvered over the obstacle course of luggage and beads. She grabbed her clothes and toiletry bag and went into the bathroom. Lisa took a shower, got dressed, and wrote on a piece of paper she took from the desk, *In the lobby,* —*L.* She left the note right next to the sink soap, so the first person to use the bathroom would see it. She quietly walked out of the hotel room into the peaceful extravagant hallway that made her feel like she was at the Palace of Versailles.

"Good morning, ma'am." Lisa heard while she was sitting on a chair in the lobby. She looked up from the newspaper she was reading to see a young, tall man standing next to her chair. He worked for the hotel. "You're up rather early. Is there something wrong with your room?"

"No, everything's fine, I just don't really sleep too much anyway and didn't want to wake my family up," Lisa responded.

"I see, can I get you anything? Coffee, tea, orange juice?"

"Tea would be great, thank you."

"Wonderful, I'll be right back," he said as he hurried away. After a few minutes, he returned with a teapot filled with hot water, an assortment of tea bags, milk, and sugar. Lisa smiled when she realized that it was a traditional English tea set up, and she didn't need to ask for milk, she felt at home.

"I grabbed this for you too," the man said as he pointed to a chocolate croissant.

"Thank you! What's your name?" Lisa asked as she opened a bag of Earl Grey and put it in the water of her tea cup to let steep for four minutes.

"Marcus, and you?"

"I'm Lisa," she said as she reached out her hand to shake his.

"Pleasure to meet you, Lisa," Marcus said as they shook hands. "Where are you from?"

"Los Angeles area, I'm here with my family. They lived in New Orleans for years but live in North Carolina now. They come back every year for Mardi Gras, so I thought I'd finally join in on the fun this year."

"Wow, Los Angeles, I've spent some time there. When I was a kid, our house got nearly destroyed from a hurricane, and my family and I stayed with my aunt who lives out there while our house was being rebuilt. We stayed there for about six months before we moved back. I sure do miss In-N-Out burger."

While she pulled the tea bag out of the cup, mixing in the milk and sugar, Lisa replied, "Yes! That's a good thing to miss. This is my first time visiting New Orleans. It's not at all what I was expecting especially since it's Mardi Gras. It's actually nicer than what I was expecting."

"Yeah, I like living here. It's not as fast-paced or exciting as LA, but I like it."

"Me too. I'd live here if my hair would be able to handle it. My curly hair and this humidity do not work well. You can sit down if you'd like," Lisa motioned to the extra chair. "How long have you been working here?"

"Thanks, ma'am, but I shouldn't sit, I'm working. I've been working here for two years. I go to Tulane, this is my last year."

"Tulane, very nice. What are you studying?"

"Sports Medicine. Are you still in school?"

"No, I graduated a few years ago. I'm just another corporate crony pushing papers and working for the man."

"Naw, you're not a crony. I see corporate cronies all the time in here, and you're not one of them. Gotta get that experience on the résumé though, right?"

"Correct. So, sports medicine, very impressive. I wish I went into medicine, but I can't handle seeing blood. Do you want to work for like a pro team or start your own practice?"

"Yeah, I applied for an internship with the Saints. Hopefully, I get an answer soon. Even interning for them would be a dream come true."

"Yeah, that would be amazing, you're like a hero to everyone, to the players, the coaches, even the people of the city will respect you for keeping the players healthy."

"Don't get my hopes too high." He laughed. "What are your plans for today?"

"Not sure, we're going to a place called the West Bank to meet up with a friend of my uncle's for lunch. Then do some shopping and get ready for some ball for the Indian parade or something."

He smiled. "You mean Endymion?"

"Right, that's it. It's hard to decipher the accent here. I promise I'm not normally this unfamiliar. I knew Cajun was its own language with its linguistic structure, but I didn't think it was that prevalent."

"Yep, here in New Orleans, we like to keep traditions alive. The West Bank is the area across the river. It's just a bunch of suburbs and houses."

"Cool, any recommendations on what to see and do in this city?"

"Well, make sure you eat a po' boy since I know you can't really get many of those out in California. Drink an Obituary, the voodoo shops are cool, creepy but still cool. But I'm pretty sure you got all your bases covered with your family. Plus, since it's Mardi Gras, you'll get the full New Orleans experience."

"What's an Obituary?" Lisa asked. She was intrigued, she had never heard of that drink before.

"Obituary is a local drink. It's a gin martini with absinthe. It's one of my favorites. Monday is my favorite day for Mardi Gras season because it's a special day of the festival called Lundi Gras. You'll see lots of the bands out that day. Well I have to go and actually get to work now," Marcus said while glancing at his watch.

"How much do I owe for this?" Lisa asked while motioning to her tea tray.

"It's on the house. Happy Mardi Gras," Marcus said as he smiled and walked toward the concierge desk.

"Why, thank you. Happy Mardi Gras," she replied. Lisa picked up the newspaper she had started reading. As she continued to read a column about the Thoth parade, she heard a familiar voice.

"Buenos días, niece," John said while walking toward Lisa from the elevator banks. "The girls are getting, they'll be down in a bit. What time did you get up?"

"I don't know. Like 6:00 AM," Lisa responded.

"Good lawd, why? Are you stressed about something or what?" John asked while sitting down in the chair facing her.

41

"I don't know, I guess since Matt and I ended things, it's been a rough transition to sleeping alone and not having him near me anymore," Lisa said while taking a sip of her tea.

"Your mom said you were handling it fine," John commented.

"Sometimes I feel fine. Sometimes I feel like I don't recognize myself," Lisa said. She was shocked at how honest she was in that moment with her uncle, it felt like the words just spilled out of her mouth.

"Yeah, I know how that goes. Luckily, you two ended things before you got married. I know what you mean about transitioning and no sleep. Bad dreams, huh?" John explained, accurately guessing the source of her lack of sleep.

"Yes, it's not fair. I'll have a great day where I don't think about him, then I'll dream about him, and it will ruin my morning," Lisa said in an annoying and defeatist tone.

"You're still in the healing phase. It takes time, but it gets easier, and the pain gets less, then before you know it, it's gone. I went through the same thing when Gabby's mom and I split up. Your mom said he was messing around with a girl who worked with him, covered in tattoos, with piercings all in her face. She sounds like a real winner. I'm sure his Stepford wife, peppy, blond conservative mother loved that. Soon he'll realize what he lost and might try to come back, but, darling, don't fall for it. As a man, trust me, a guy like that is low-grade garbage. A guy like that is not worth taking back, not even as a friend. He'll do it again the minute the opportunity presents itself."

Lisa chuckled then took a sip of her tea. She was surprised because she felt a tinge of repulsion at the idea of taking him back and kissing him again.

"God, if he even does try to come back, the trust is gone. He looked into my face, stared at me directly into my eyes, and lied. I for sure don't want that in my life in any capacity. Hopefully, he won't even think about trying to come back to my life."

"Good, let time go by then you'll know that you deserve a man that is so much better than him," John said with a nod.

Lisa smiled. "Thanks, Uncle Johnny."

"Anytime, kiddo. Now, where is my wife and daughter?" John said while unlocking his phone to make a phone call. "Hey, we're hungry, how much longer y'all gonna be?" John said in a hangry tone. "Okay, see you soon," John said. He took the phone away from his ear and pressed the end button. "They're in the elevator."

Right as John motioned to the elevator, the door opened, and both Gabby and Joan walked out toward John and Lisa. They walked slowly and looked tired. Gabby was already wearing her sunglasses. She looked like a pop star trying to be incognito. When they got closer to John and Lisa, with a smile, Joan simply said, "Morning. Mother's?"

# CHAPTER 7

## *Mother's*

"WHAT'S MOTHER'S?" LISA asked while trying to keep up with her fast-walking family as they hurried through the hotel lobby toward the gold exit doors.

"Mother's is one of my all-time favorite restaurants in New Orleans. I can't wait to get a crawfish etouffee omelet," John said in a tone of anxiousness and nostalgia. As they approached the golden doors of the lobby, the doorman opened and smiled at Lisa and her family.

"Good morning," the doorman said as he opened the door.

"Morning, sir, thank you," John said as he and Joan exited the doors first.

Lisa and Gabby followed saying good morning and exchanging greetings with the doorman as they made their way onto the damp and dewy morning streets of New Orleans. The air was crisp with a slight breeze. A haze was slowly lifting out of the city that made it look like the city itself was hungover. Lisa and her family came to a busy intersection, standing at a crosswalk waiting for the walking signal.

Lisa looked around at the downtown cityscape before her of skyscrapers and streetcar lines. The cover of the previous night hid the beauty of the architecture New Orleans was famous for. She was pleasantly surprised at the cleanliness of the streets.

"You would never guess that this place was trashed and covered in beads just a few hours ago," Lisa acknowledged.

"Mardi Gras has been going on for over a century. They got parading and the cleanup down to a science out here," John responded as he impatiently hit the walk button. "Yeah, the only beads you see are the ones that get stuck in the trees, the streetcar lines and streetlamps. Come Monday, there's gonna be a lot more beads stuck in the trees, the branches are gonna be weighted down."

The streetlight turned, and gave the signal to walk across. As soon as they crossed the street, the sign came into full view, *Mother's Restaurant est. 1938*. The restaurant was housed in a large brick building that dominated the street but still looked like a true hole in the wall. They walked into the historic diner with pictures, newspaper articles, magazine covers, awards, and pictures of celebrities everywhere.

The hostess first greeted the Perez family with a smile and said, "Good morning. Four?"

"Good morning! Yes, ma'am, table for four, please," Joan responded.

"Excellent, follow me," the hostess said while grabbing a stack of menus. The hostess escorted them to a round, circular table that could sit a lot more than four people. Gabby handed Lisa a menu, and the first thing she noticed in the breakfast section was crawfish etouffee.

Perplexed, Lisa asked, "What's crawfish etouffee?"

"It's like a sauce with crawfish they put over the omelet," Joan responded.

"It's delicious," John chimed in.

"Do you like crawfish?" Joan asked Lisa.

"Never tried it, but, hey, I'll give it a try now."

"I just want a regular omelet with biscuits. I remember the biscuits here, they're so good," Gabby said while closing the menu.

"Must be, since you had to have been around eight the last time you were here," John responded.

"Morning, are y'all ready to order?" the waitress asked as she approached the table.

"Yeah, I'll take a crawfish etouffee and a cup of chicory coffee," Joan said.

Lisa could tell that Joan was excited to eat this meal. She ordered the omelet with a sense of urgency, as if she were afraid the restaurant would run out of etouffee sauce.

"Same here, except I'll take regular coffee," John said.

"I'll have the same as him with the etouffee and regular coffee," Lisa ordered.

"I'll take a regular cheese omelet with a biscuit," Gabby said.

"All omelets come with a biscuit, ma'am, do you want an extra?" the waitress informed Gabby.

"Oh, it comes with one? Great, no extra one. I'll just take the one it comes with. I'll get a regular coffee as well, please," Gabby said while handing her menu to the waitress.

Lisa looked around the restaurant that was already starting to get crowded. The walls were lined with pictures of famous people and their autographs, as well as newspaper articles from the *Times Picayune*. Lisa admired the pride and the history that the restaurant humble-bragged, which made her even more curious to try the food at the famed foodie's paradise. The waitress returned balancing a tray of coffees. She gave Joan the chicory coffee first, as to not forget which cup had the different coffee in it. Then handed out the three regular coffees. The family reached toward the middle of the table where the creamer containers and sugar packets were, to make their coffees to their exact likings. Lisa heard a beautiful voice singing from the restaurant, she curiously looked around to see who was singing, until she realized it was coming from the kitchen.

KITCHEN. Down in New Orleans where the where the blues was born,
     the combo's there with a mambo beat Mardi Gras mambo.
JOHN, *soft tone*. Mambo, mambo.
KITCHEN. Mardi Gras mambo.
JOHN, *soft tone*. Mambo, mambo.

"Are you singing?" Lisa asked curiously.

"This song is a classic. When someone sings 'Mardi Gras Mambo,' you respond 'Mambo, mambo,'" John said to Lisa with attitude as if it were common knowledge.

KITCHEN. Mardi Gras mambo.

JOHN, *louder voice*. Mambo, mambo.

KITCHEN, *louder*. Mardi Gras mambo.

JOHN, JOAN, LISA, GABBY. Mambo, mambo.

KITCHEN AND A FEW OTHERS IN THE RESTAURANT. Mardi Gras
  mambo, ohhhh.

EVERYONE IN THE RESTAURANT. Down in New Orleans.

The waitress approached the table with their breakfast, unfazed by the impromptu singing in the restaurant. "Crawfish etouffee, omelet, biscuit basket. Do y'all need anything else?"

"Nope, I think we're good, thank you," Joan said with a smile.

"Enjoy your breakfast, y'all," the waitress said as she smiled and walked away.

"Okay, home chicken, how do you like it?" John asked Lisa.

Lisa stared at the omelet that was covered in a brown-red sauce, it looked like gumbo but instead of shrimp there was only small chunks of crawfish. She was a bit apprehensive at first since she is not one for odd-textured food. She grabbed the fork and took a bite. The roux was seasoned perfectly, not too spicy, not too sweet, with a hint of tomato; it was unlike anything she had ever tasted before. The crawfish had absorbed the spices like a sponge. The buttery roux base and the buttery omelet were a great base to have in common, while the spices provided the perfect contrast to a regular omelet. Lisa's family watched for a reaction and ruling to this new type of food she was about to try.

"It's delicious!" Lisa said after she took her first bite.

"Ahh, lovely," John said while proceeding to eat his omelet.

"After breakfast, I say we head to the French Quarter and do a little shopping to kill time before we catch the ferry to the West

Bank. If we're lucky, we may be able to come across a walking parade or two," Joan explained.

"Can we drop by the voodoo store? I want to get a voodoo doll for my friend," Gabby asked.

"Sure," John replied, half listening and enjoying his omelet.

"Did you guys eat here all the time when you lived here?" Lisa asked her aunt and uncle.

"Oh yeah, this place is a historical landmark. We'd come here for breakfast and for po' boys. I've seen more famous people eating here than I ever did when I lived in LA," Joan responded.

"Yeah, J, remember when we were here last time and Emeril Legassee came in? We thought he looked familiar, but we just kept minding our business because we weren't sure. Then he came over and started asking about my shirt, which was from a country club I belonged to when we lived in Cape May, and that's when it clicked that it was him."

"Yeah, one time I was standing right at that counter ordering a po' boy to go when Harry Connick Jr. walked in and orders a po' boy. He's so handsome, he always comes for Mardi Gras, his krewe puts on the Orpheus parade. Orpheus and Bacchus are the ones with the celebrities," Joan said.

"I read that Will Farrell is going to be the king of Bacchus this year," Gabby said.

"I love him!" Lisa responded. "I hope I run into him on the street. I just want to give him a hug and tell him to stay classy."

They were all equally amused, laughed, and enjoyed their breakfast the way all families laugh and enjoy a meal together. Lisa loved laughing with her family; she was also glad that the reputation of the restaurant lived up to the hype and highly set expectations. After John settled the bill and the plates were removed from the table, they stood up and started walking out the door. As soon as they exited the restaurant, a line was starting to form down the street. The sight of people queueing to get into the restaurant reminded Lisa of a club in Hollywood. Now Lisa understood why Joan and John go to the restaurant as early as possible to avoid lines.

"I'm going back to the hotel and take a nap before we go. I'll meet y'all at the ferry, okay?" John said before kissing Joan.

"Okay, see you at the ferry," Joan responded.

John walked in the direction toward the hotel while Joan, Gabby, and Lisa started walking toward the French Quarter.

The city and Lisa were officially awake. She had eaten a great breakfast, and the caffeine had kicked in. The sun was out as well as the people. It was the Saturday before Mardi Gras. Artists, musicians, performers, every street performer, and panhandler were out on the street trying to make a buck. Joan, Gabby, and Lisa were walking around the French Quarter enjoying the sights and the entertainment while other people were throwing beads off and onto balconies like they were playing game of catch. The buildings were colorful and adorned with intricate iron designs on the balconies locals refer to as French lace. Most of the balconies were decorated with Mardi Gras decorations.

"The color of these shutters on the buildings is a very unique color and only mixed here, it's called French Quarter green," Joan said as she pointed out the shutters on one of the buildings. They slowly walked on the sidewalk, careful to not run into a post, over the uneven pavement, trying not to trip in a pothole while also avoiding the drips coming from the balconies.

"One of the tricks some of the con artists play here is they'll come up to you and say, 'Five bucks and I'll tell you where your shoes are.' And usually tourists will be like, 'Umm, okay, they're on my feet.' The con artists will say, 'They're on your feet on Bourbon Street.' Then they'll get mad at you and not leave you alone until you pay up. So, if someone comes up to you and asks where are your shoes, you say, 'I'm a local, leave me alone' or 'They're on my feet on Bourbon Street.' Pretty much if anyone tries to hassle, you say 'I'm a local, leave me alone' then they back off," Joan educated Lisa and Gabby on her local street knowledge as they were walking, Gabby to her right and Lisa following closely since the sidewalks were too narrow for all three to walk next to each other.

"Sounds like San Francisco. The trick there is to just keep walking, don't stand in one place for too long because someone will come up to you and try to pull a fast one or at least ask for spare change. Did you ever come here when you were in college for Mardi Gras, Aunt Joan?"

"I did once with a group of friends, but I was too poor in college, so my fun was limited. But yeah, that was a good quick trip. The most fun we had was the drive here from Florida. When you're in college and you don't really know much of the area, you go to Bourbon Street, which as you saw from yesterday, is not quite the place you want to spend the whole time, ya know. But now that I've lived here, I know where to go. I just miss it so much at times too because it's easy to fall in love with this city. Remember Vivian from the wedding?"

"Yes, I remember Viv."

"She lives over on the West Bank, she's coming to the parades tonight."

"Oh, awesome, I liked her when I met her at your wedding. Wow, look at this place," Lisa said as they walked in front of a store filled with Mardi Gras masks.

"Let's go in, you'll need one for tonight," Joan said while walking toward the entrance of the store.

The store was filled with feathers and glitter galore. If a patron had an allergy to feathers, they would probably break out in a small rash just by walking past the entrance. The ladies walked in and immediately started to try on the masks. They examined how they looked in the mirrors posted throughout the store.

"Joan, can I get this one? It will go perfect with my outfit tonight," Gabby said while holding a pink-and-gold mask to her face.

"Gabs, your dress is green."

"I know, but it's Mardi Gras! It's okay if things don't match if you can pull it off, and I totally can pull this off," Gabby said while continuing to hold the mask to her face.

"What color is your dress, Lisa?" Joan asked while holding a black mask to her face.

"Just a long black dress."

"Perfect, then you can practically choose whatever mask you want," Joan said while holding a turquoise mask to her face.

"I like this one," Lisa said while holding a purple mask to her face with purple feathers, gold glitter, adorned with green-and-gold rhinestones. It looked regal; it sparkled like a fresh polished diamond no matter what lighting it was in. She found the mask that she was looking for. Lisa found the mask that she would make her official Mardi Gras debut in.

"All sorted?" Joan asked before putting the mask she was to buy for Gabby on the counter to pay.

"Yep, I'm ready for the ball," Lisa said as she did a twirl in the direction of the checkout line.

Lisa felt giddy and excited. She hadn't been to a formal event since college. She always enjoyed getting glamourous and dressing for nice events. She was even more excited that she didn't have to worry about bruising her ex's ego by being taller than him. After seeing the formal dresses from last night, she knew that she was going to experience something unique.

# CHAPTER 8

## *West Bank*

LISA FOLLOWED JOAN and Gabby's lead into the gray building of steel and cement that was devoid of Mardi Gras decorations or any character whatsoever. The Canal Street ferry building was crowded with people arriving to the city for Mardi Gras festivities. Lisa and her family were part of the small number of passengers leaving the city. Lisa spotted John leaning against the railings of the entrance to the ferry patiently waiting for them. He had already purchased their round-trip tickets.

"Hello, wife," John said as he embraced Joan and gave her a quick kiss. "Hey, girls," he said to Lisa and Gabby. John led the way onto the boat. He gave their ticket to the attendant who used a hole punch to mark the ticket then returned it to John. They walked onto the ferry and grabbed seats on two benches facing each other on the stern of the ship. The air was cold, but the sun was shining, which made for a nice trip across the river.

"Did y'all get anything good?" John asked Gabby.

"We bought masks for tonight," Gabby responded, opening the bag to show John the masks.

"Lovely," John said as he casually glanced inside the bag.

As they began their journey across the Mississippi River, Lisa looked out across the vast choppy river; she could see the current moving quickly ahead of the boat. She asked, "Do people ever swim in the Mississippi?"

"No way, never, this river is very dangerous," John quickly responded as he looked out at the river.

"I've never pulled anyone out of this thing alive. Especially in this stretch with all of the boats," Joan chimed in. As members of the Coast Guard, both Joan and John have been part of many search and rescue missions.

"Why do they call that the West Bank?" Lisa asked Joan as she motioned to the body of land they were heading toward.

"I'm not sure because technically, the two areas are north and south," Joan responded.

"So, what's over there?" Lisa asked, "Is it still part of New Orleans?"

"Just some houses, the suburbs. Our friends live in a town over there called Gretna."

Lisa stared out onto the river. She had never seen a river so wide. A gust of wind made Lisa immediately button up her coat to combat the cold air. She could tell that the water was freezing cold because the temperature dropped significantly as soon as they reached the midpoint of the river.

As the ferry docked and they walked off the boat, Lisa turned around to gaze across the river to look at the city. The city looked calm and peaceful. St. Louis Cathedral looked small but still retained its beauty and dominance. There were patches of sunlight shining on parts of the city as if certain sections were entitled to the light and others were kept in the dark. Lisa turned around and noticed that her family was now quite a bit of distance ahead of her. She hurried to catch up with them. They were walking toward a brown building with a slate roof and wraparound porch; a large red sign hung over the entry read ZYDECO's in large block letters. As they entered the restaurant, Lisa was surprised to see how empty it was. They had arrived just before the lunch rush. There was a large sign in the foyer that read PLEASE SEAT YOURSELF. John had picked out a large table in the middle of the restaurant. The decor was gaudy with alligator figurines and New Orleans Saints football signs everywhere. Every campy decoration was given an extra bit of tackiness and Mardi Gras spirit. Mardi Gras beads covered everything that a bead could be strung across.

After a few minutes of sitting at the table and glancing at the menu, Lisa heard John say, "There he is." John stood up to greet his friend, Dan, with a handshake and a hug. "How are you, Kimmy?" John said while giving Dan's wife, Kim, a hug. Joan stood up and greeted them with a hug as well.

"Lisa, these are our dear friends, Dan and Kim Dessault. We've known each other for years," Joan said. "Guys, this is our niece. She came to visit New Orleans from California for Mardi Gras. We're giving her the VIP treatment."

"Nice to meet you," Dan said while holding out his hand to shake Lisa's.

"Nice to meet you both," Lisa said while shaking both Kim and Dan's hands.

"You remember Gabby, right?" John said while motioning to his daughter.

"Of course, you got a little taller but still look the same since we last saw you years back. How old are you now, honey?" Kim asked.

"Seventeen," Gabby responded while shaking hands with Dan and Kim.

"Wow, you're getting old," Dan joked. "What about you, Lisa, what part of California are you from?" Dan asked Lisa.

"Los Angeles area," Lisa responded.

"Oh, LA fun, we have a house in San Clemente. We love Southern California most of the time. I wish there wasn't so much traffic though."

"Yeah, that's the biggest downside."

"I was also shocked at how cold that ocean was. When I was in the Marines, I got so excited when I was told I was going to be stationed in San Diego. I'm a swamp kid, so I was hoping to learn to surf and live the endless summer life. But oh lawd, the water in that Pacific is freezing! We'd have to do drills and trainings in that water, it was borderline torture. I guess it's a good strategy for making soldiers. I don't think I intentionally swam in there more than a few times in the four years I lived there," Dan said before opening the menu.

"Yep, the water is always cold in California. It's because the current comes from Alaska. It's also why we never get hurricanes because the water is too cold for a storm of that magnitude. I mainly avoid swimming in the ocean because I know I'll get eaten by a shark." Lisa added, "I'll paddleboard in the harbor, but swimming and surfing are not for me."

"I don't need swimming when we go out to the West Coast either. Just put me on the beach with a good bottle of wine and I'm in heaven," Kim said before taking a sip of water.

"Hello, welcome to Zydeco's. Are y'all ready to order?" the waitress asked as she warmly smiled as if they were guests in her house.

As Lisa read the menu, she noticed an ingredient listed that she never saw before, quizzically, she asked, "What's trinity spice?"

Joan smirked. "Onion, bell pepper, celery. The basis to all creole dishes."

"Okay, interesting," Lisa said, still not entirely sure the meaning and how it pertained to a po' boy shrimp sandwich. One by one, the whole table gave their orders. One by one, they all ordered dressed shrimp po' boy sandwiches; Lisa followed the crowd and ordered the same.

"So, how you feeling, Dan?" John asked before taking a drink of his Abita.

"Doing better. I'm feeling stronger every day. I had a doctor's appointment Tuesday, and he said my heart is healthy," Dan happily responded.

"What about your leg?" Joan asked.

"Oh, that's fine, all the bed rest from the heart attack made it heal quick."

"Yeah, this whole situation is one giant press for him to finally slow down," Kim said while glaring at her husband to emphasize slow down.

"I am fifty years old, why do I need to slow down? I'm just counting my blessings and making better choices," Dan responded with confidence.

Unamused, Kim quickly shot back, "You fell off a ladder the other day."

"Yeah, but it wasn't too far, just tuck and roll."

Curious to learn more, Lisa asked, "How long ago was your heart attack?"

"Six months, before that, I hurt my leg chasing a guy, I'm a semiretired cop," Dan responded.

"Yeah, he had hurt his leg but thought he was feeling better," Kim said in a retelling of the events of Dan's heart attack. "He received an e-mail from the department saying they needed extra help for the voodoo festival, naturally Dan volunteered without hesitation. When he told me, I said no way because he was still walking funny and his knee was a bit swollen. I said you need to get a written note from your doctor and maybe you can go. He goes to the doctor and comes home with a note. Knowing him, he bribed the doctor into writing it. That night, he started complaining about being dizzy. I started having a bad feeling, so I talked him into going to the hospital. As soon as we checked him in, a heart attack hits him right there in the waiting room. If we hadn't of already been at the hospital, he would've died," Kim said with a serious look on her face.

"Yeah, I guess you saved my life, my love," Dan said as he looked at his wife adoringly.

Lisa smiled and was pleased to see their love and partnership. She got the impression by the way they looked at each other that the experience of nearly losing each other made them closer together.

The waitress arrived to their table with a tray of food. Lisa looked at the large sandwich that overflowed with lettuce, tomatoes, and fried shrimp. She was hesitant at first, but as soon as she took a bite of her po' boy, with the snap of the fresh lettuce and freshly baked baguette, she knew she made the right choice with her order. The ting and taste of the dressing sauce combined with the perfected battering of trinity spices was heavenly. The lettuce, tomato, and homemade bread made all of the odd ingredients perform like a perfectly conducted symphony. It was a combination that she wanted to savor and pinpoint every flavor like she was eating at a Michelin-starred restaurant. The food tasted delicious; she felt impressed by this simple restaurant and felt like it equated to any highly rated restaurant she ate at in Beverly Hills.

"How are y'all liking North Carolina?" Kim asked.

"It's okay, it's good to be closer to our family and all, but, man, we are surrounded by some serious rednecks though. Maybe we just lived in New Jersey for too long, but I cannot remember when the last time I saw so much nonmilitary folk wearing camo," John responded.

"Yeah, it's prime for people watching," Joan chimed in.

"Yeah, Mr. Retirement, how are you getting along with that?" Dan asked John.

"It's all right, the move has kept me busy and workin' hard," John said.

"Busy workin' hard?" Joan repeated in a sarcastic tone.

"Hey, I work very hard okay, buildin' you a patio and takin' care of the dogs and showering you with gifts," John explained while trying to maintain a serious face. Everyone else at the table was giggling.

"Yeah, Mr. Man Wife. Do you wear an apron around the house now too, Mrs. Draper?" Dan said in an attempt to troll John. Joan smiled, everyone chuckled, John grinned out of confusion.

"Don't listen to him," Kim said in defense of John. "We have a strict no-trolling policy at home now. Even at work, he's not allowed to troll anymore. So, he's getting it out of his system while he can."

"Oh dang, you must've been super bad to have an intervention pulled on you," Gabby responded.

"Yeah, at first I couldn't do it at work. Then it was all built up all day, and I'd come home and give it to Kim," Dan said.

"And you better believe I shut that down real quick. I instituted the no-trolling policy at home," Kim said in an authoritative tone.

"Y'all are hilarious. John has his moments, but no interventions are needed just yet," Joan said while laughing.

"So, Lisa, what do you do? Work? School?" Dan asked.

"Just work. I'm sort of seeing where life leads me, I guess. But I'm getting the itch to go to grad school. I've been slowly researching those options. One of the concierges at the hotel goes to Tulane and was telling me about his sports medicine program this morning. Maybe Tulane could be an option for grad school," Lisa said.

"What are you looking to study?" Kim asked.

"I'm not sure. Maybe just get my MBA. Since I'm not married and no kids, I might as well do it while I have the time," Lisa said.

"What's your bachelors in?" Dan asked.

"Literature, my life is a big ball of irony. I studied English literature, but now I work in tech," Lisa said as she shrugged her shoulders.

"You know, I read that Steve Jobs would hire philosophy majors and other majors that were not exclusively in business or technology. He said that it helped with generating innovation and creativity. So, I think it's great that you are in an environment that you can use all aspects of your brain. It also shows your courage and curiosity. Our niece has been looking for a job for two years. For some reason, she thinks she's going to get her dream job, but no one gets their dream job at twenty-two. You just need to do something for your résumé and get your life going."

"Yeah, that's so true, and I've seen that a lot with some of my friends who think they can be picky with their careers when they're just entry level. I tell them that they just need to take the scraps that are given to them. Everyone needs to prove their worth first. Then you can be picky when you really know what you can handle and what you want to do," Lisa said.

"Amen to that," Dan responded. "So, when does y'all's plane take off?"

"Monday morning, but Lisa's plane doesn't leave until Monday evening. Y'all have any ideas what she could do during the day?" John said.

"Lundi Gras," Kim said with her hand slightly raised as if a lightbulb turned on in her head.

"That's right, I forgot about that," Joan commented.

"What's Lundi Gras?" Gabby asked curiously.

"The festivities for the day before Mardi Gras. It's all music focused and more Zulu influenced. It's a cool and fun time. Every band and musician are out in the streets playing for money, and the riverfront park by the mall and that ferry dock we came here on, it will have a big stage set up for concerts. Then at night, king of carnival named Rex arrives and shakes hands with the Zulu king to create peace for Fat Tuesday. It's a big thing and lots of fun," Joan said before taking another bite of her po' boy.

"That's actually when we plan on heading into the city and hear some of the local bands play," Kim added.

"Yeah, what are y'all doing tonight?" Joan asked, "We can get you tickets to the St. Charles ball."

"Oh, y'all are so kind," Kim replied, "but our son is coming home tonight with his college friends to party, so I need to prepare the house for fifteen, twenty-one-year-olds' staying this weekend."

"Perfect specimens for me to troll!" Dan declared while rubbing his hands together like he was plotting something.

"That's awesome," Gabby said. "Is he cute? Can I see a picture?"

"He's twenty-one years old, young lady," John said.

"Where does he go to school?" Gabby asked.

"Tennessee, he's studying finance. We also have a daughter that's probably around your age, Gabby," Kim said while pulling out her phone to show pictures of her kids like every proud mother.

The picture was recent, it was their Christmas family portrait. Their daughter had thick chestnut brown hair that rivaled Kate Middleton's. She was fair-skinned with friendly hazel eyes. She took after her father more than her mother. She looked short in stature, but she looked athletic and was holding the family dog like a parent holds a baby.

"She's so beautiful," Lisa commented.

"Let me see," Gabby said while holding out her hand.

"Has she been in any parades as a queen or maid?" Joan asked.

"Not yet, she's waiting until she's a senior. It's pretty exhausting, and you want to do it when you're already on top, ya know?" Kim said while Gabby handed her phone back.

"Kim, you're from here?" John asked surprised.

"Yep, born and raised in Gretna. I was a maid during Bacchus when I was a senior in high school. It was one of the most exciting yet most exhausting days of my life," Kim said while putting her phone back into her purse.

They continued to spend the better part of an hour finishing their food. They reminisced the past, discussed the current hopes, and made future plans. They all laughed and enjoyed finishing up their po' boys. They established a bond in which the day itself would be a memory for them to reminisce with fondness in the future.

"Well that was good, but we should be getting back to the city, there's only one bathroom, four people, and three ladies to get ready for a formal ball. Baby, can you check the parade app so we know which roads will already be blocked off?" Joan asked John.

"Yeah, I'll do it on the boat," John said as he quickly took out cash from his wallet to cover the entire bill and gave it to the waitress without letting Dan see or help pay.

"My treat," John said while giving Dan a smile.

"Aight, I'll let you get this one, Perez, thank you," Dan said as he lifted his beer to cheers John.

They all got up from their seats and walked out of the restaurant that had just slightly more patrons than there was when the family arrived. They all gave each other hugs and said their goodbyes. Kim and Dan walked toward the parking lot where their truck was parked. Lisa and her family walked to the dock right in time to catch the next ferry across to the city.

As they boarded the boat and began to sail across the Mississippi River, Joan stood at the stern, gazing at the bridge next to them. Lisa walked over to join her and take in the city views from the ferry. As she looked across the massive river, Lisa thought about the last two hours at lunch with Dan and Kim. She enjoyed the lively lunchtime conversations with Kim and Dan. She enjoyed learning more about the city and the stories of its residents. Out of all the places in the world she had traveled, she felt welcome by everyone she had met. After months of feeling rejected, she was happy to feel accepted.

In a sigh of content and nostalgia, Joan said, "I love this city. It was such a pivotal moment in my life when I lived here. It was the combination of adopting my old dog, Buster, remember him?"

"Yeah, I loved Buster," Lisa said, smiling, remembering the dog with fondness.

Lisa felt the rays of light warm her face as she stared up into the opalescent sky. The breeze moved her hair as she stood next to Joan on the boat having this mother-daughter type moment of reflection and healing while they sailed across the river that held just as many hopes, dreams, traumas, and failures that both Joan and Lisa could resonate with.

"Yeah, he was great. Adopting him and the friendly people in this city, is what helped me get through my divorce and allowed the healing to get me in the right mindset for when I met your uncle. Even one of our first dates was jogging along the banks of this river while we were both living here. I know the pain you have with what Matt did to you. I recognize and sympathize with everything you are going through. I heard you get up this morning, it was 4:00 AM in California, so it's not like it's your internal clock that got you up," Joan said in a concerned tone.

Lisa was not herself, and even family she rarely saw noticed in the twenty-four hours she had been around them. In that moment, Lisa knew she needed to be transparent with Joan. She could not fake being fine like she had been doing with her friends and coworkers. Lisa took a deep breath then replied, "The anger is gone, the pain is a little less every day. The hardest part is the memories. The ghost that was our relationship haunts my dreams. I'll have a good day then as soon as I go to sleep, I'll dream about him or see his face in a dream. Then I'll wake up sad, and sometimes, I'll wake up so early that I'm terrified to go back to sleep. I wish I could control my dreams."

"Well, I don't know how to control dreams, but I do know that we only dream about the faces we've seen. So, because you've seen his face so many times for so many years, of course, your mind will default to him. The only way to combat that is to make new memories and meet new people. I can't tell you when you'll be ready to date again, but I can tell you that when you walk into a room, people notice you, all heads turn, guys look at you. But you still give the impression of not interested. You have a beautiful smile, you can make someone's day by just giving them a smile. You are that beautiful person who can make someone feel good by just being nice to them. Who knows, a simple, 'good morning' could give the guy courage to approach you."

"I just wish that I knew guys are good, ya know. It's like right when I feel like destiny has finally quit giving me the middle finger by giving me someone nice, it's like psyche, fooled you again! How did you bounce back, Aunt Joan? I feel like you are one of the few people I know who can relate to what happened."

"The only thing that truly worked on me was taking it one day at a time. It's weird and a bit cliché, but it's true. One thing I did was at the end of the night while lying in bed, I would give thanks for the good that happened during that day. Even if the only good thing was having a roof over my head and food in my kitchen. It takes practice and being intentional, but it works, and soon you appreciate the littlest things and become more aware of who you are. When you truly know yourself is when it's officially safe to let others in. It also lessens the hurt because you know what's right for you, and what you want, and what you don't want."

"I just want to be happy again. I don't feel like myself anymore. I feel like there's a piece of me that is missing. I honestly can't remember myself before Matt. I don't think I know how to even figure out what that missing piece is. It scares me, it really does. I've had moments like this before, but never this long. Never this intense. It's like the hole is too deep and I can't get out. It's like I've become addicted to the sadness."

"I think what you should do is try to focus on being the woman you want to be. Then in the process, it will manifest itself. Do you think you need to see a therapist or someone?" Joan asked.

"I don't know, that's one of the reasons why I wanted to come here. I wanted to have a new experience. Maybe a new experience will help me feel something again. If I don't feel anything different, if I don't feel that lust for life like I did before, then I'll call a therapist. But I think it has been working. Last night I felt happy, last night I felt at peace, and I felt like myself," Lisa said.

"If you need anything like money to pay for it or whatever, I'll pay for it, don't worry, darling. But I think that's a good strategy. Like I said, it was this city and Buster that helped me. So, I get what your strategy is, and I hope it does work. We're here for you, and we love you," Joan said in earnest.

With a single tear escaping Lisa's tough visage, she said, "Thank you, Aunt Joan."

"Aww, I love you, darlin'," Joan said as she wrapped one arm around Lisa, cuddling her. "It gets better, I promise. Plus, tonight is going to be amazing, trust me."

"Good, I'm excited because if you consider it amazing, then I know it will truly be amazing," Lisa replied.

The water was calm and the sun was shining. Lisa felt like a weight had been lifted off her shoulders; Joan was the first person in her life she told exactly how she was feeling and how deep the pain went. Lisa felt new, she felt empowered. The passing through the river felt like a passing through time. Lisa felt like she went through an emotional barrier and the problems were left in the river and she had made it through to the other side to freedom. She felt lucky that she had her aunt who had been through worse be able to relate to her heartbreak and counsel her. The buildings were slowly getting bigger as the boat approached the city. As they got closer, the music from the *Steamboat Natchez* was becoming more audible. As she got closer, she was able to recognize the song coming from the steam pipes. It was playing the state song "You Are My Sunshine" through its steam organ like it was welcoming the ferry boat back to the city. For the first time in a long time, Lisa felt motivated and excited to go to the ball and hopefully find her missing piece.

⚜

"Babe, can you help me tie my bow?" John hollered from the main room.

The three women had commandeered the bathroom mirror to do their hair and makeup for the masquerade ball. "Yeah, one sec," Joan hollered while applying her mascara. After one last swipe of the mascara wand, Joan put her mascara back into her makeup bag then exited the bathroom to assist John.

"All right, I'm ready!" Gabby announced after applying high-lighter to her cheeks. "Can you help me with the hook on my dress, Lis?" Gabby asked Lisa while taking off her bathrobe and adjusting the green strapless ball gown she was wearing under it. Just as Lisa was about to hook Gabby's dress, she noticed bruising on Gabby's back and a bandage that looked like it was covering a large part of her torso.

"Gabs, what is this on your side?" Lisa asked Gabby, concerned and confused at what looked to be a wound.

"Nothing!" Gabby said while quickly turning away from Lisa, embarrassed and fearful.

"Is that a..."

"Shhh!" Gabby said, flustered.

"What is that?" Lisa whispered in an authoritative tone.

"Shh! Okay, I was at a party, and this guy had different brands, so I let him brand me."

Lisa's eyes opened wide with shock and anger. "What the!" Lisa said loudly. She caught herself before she said anymore. "Okay, why?" she asked her cousin calmly but sternly while she made very harsh and direct eye contact.

"I don't know, it's a peace sign, cool, huh?" Gabby replied as she smiled sheepishly and made a peace sign with her fingers.

"No, that is not cool. A branded peace sign is not cool. Brands were reserved for slaves and cattle. You are no one's slave, and you're not a piece of meat. Don't ever let anyone do that to you again. I mean come on, you're only seventeen, if you want to be rebellious, get something that can be removed like a piercing or a tattoo. Brands are forever, dude." Lisa felt saddened and disappointed in Gabby. She'd heard about some of Gabby's rebellious acts, but she didn't think it would lead to being branded.

"Can you just hook my dress, please?" Gabby said as she turned her back to Lisa. Lisa hooked her dress quickly, and Gabby stormed out of the bathroom just as Joan returned.

"What's her problem?" Joan said as she walked back into the bathroom to put on blush, the last part of her makeup routine.

"Teenagers," Lisa responded as she rolled her eyes.

"That girl, she gets some crazy moods," Joan commented while she applied blush to the apples of her cheeks. "Are you excited for tonight?"

"Yes, I haven't been to a formal event in years. Well at least one where drinking heavily is encouraged. I generally don't get drunk at weddings," Lisa said as she took the mascara wand out of the bottle.

Joan chuckled. "If I didn't know you better, I'd be nervous. But I know you can handle your liquor. Okay, now I'm ready. I'm going to go and put on my shoes and coat," Joan said after she gave herself one last look over in the mirror.

"Cool, I'm almost ready."

Lisa put the final touches of lipstick on. She sprayed perfume on her wrists and a spritz in her hair. Lisa looked at her mask as it laid in front of her on the vanity. The lighting of the bathroom gave the glitter and rhinestones an iridescent glow that made the mask look like it was moving in a mischievous way. The gold glowed along the rim as if it were protecting the rich green and regal purple rhinestones of the inner part of the mask. She adjusted the straps of her black gown; a bridesmaid dress she never thought she would wear again but was happy that the price per wear ratio was evening out. She picked up the mask and held it to her face. Lisa felt confident, sexy, and flirty. The heat of her skin and the cold of the plastic caused her face to nearly fuse together with the mask. Once she got a decent fit, she tied the ribbon on the back of her head to secure the mask. Lisa felt as sexy and playful as the mask looked.

*Click, click, click,* she heard as she walked into the main room. John and his friend, Steve, were engaged in a sword fight with the scepters John made of wood, glitter, and beads from previous Mardi Gras throws. They were both wearing tuxedos that James Bond would be proud of, but instead of top hats, they wore green, gold, and purple jester hats.

"What in the world is goin' on in here?" Lisa commented as she walked out into the main room, confused at the spectacle but nonetheless entertained.

"Hey, Lis, you remember my best friend, Vivian?" Joan asked while motioning toward Vivian who was sitting on the bed next to her.

"Yes, of course. It's great to see you again," Lisa said while she walked across the room to hug Vivian.

"It's good to see you too. You look great! It's good to see you embracing our culture. As you can tell, it's not taken lightly here," Vivian said as she motioned to the men fencing with the scepters. Vivian looked radiant. She wore a gold dress with gold elbow-length gloves, partnered with a gold mask that made her look like an Oscar statue.

When the men stopped their sword fight, John introduced Steve to Lisa.

"Steve, this is our lovely niece, Lisa, or Lis is another nickname we have for her," John said as he pointed his scepter to Lisa. He had small beads of sweat on his nose and brow and was short of breath from the few minutes of fencing.

"How do you do, mademoiselle?" Steve said as he bowed down to her, still in character as a chivalrous jester. Steve was extremely tall and towered over everyone, the jester hat added another foot to his already tall stature.

"It's good to see you're doing something productive with your time in retirement, John," Vivian said as she gestured toward the scepters. John chuckled as he twirled the scepter like a baseball player on deck.

"Yeah, when he found out y'all were coming to the ball, he ran out to the arts-and-craft store to make these scepters. It was funny seeing him at his workbench that is usually covered with tools and saws get covered with beads, gemstones, and glitter. His workbench looked like a scene from *RuPaul's Drag Race*," Joan said, giggling.

"Well, they look fabulous," Vivian replied.

"I challenge you to a duel!" Steve shouted as he assumed the fencing position in front of John.

"Challenge accepted!" John said as he assumed his position, ready to fence again.

"Okay, boys!" Joan intervened. "The car should be here by now. We gotta go before they start blocking off the street and have to miss dinner."

"To be continued," John said to Steve while still in position and giving a slight nod of his head. Steve smiled and nodded his head in response.

"Okay, let's go. Here, baby, hold our tickets," Joan said as she handed John the tickets. She grabbed her coat and wristlet and ushered everyone out of the room.

The lobby was a festival and spectacle of people as they hurried about the lobby, trying to get outside to their optimal parade viewing locations. All six of them jumped into the van and were quickly whisked away to the St. Charles Hotel for the Endymion Armed Forces Ball.

# CHAPTER 9

## *La Mascarade*

CROWDS LINED THE streets, camped out with folding chairs and coolers, an entire city tailgated as they were drunkenly yet patiently waiting for the parade to arrive. The van that Lisa and her family rode in caught the small window of street availability and steadily cut through the intersection like a knife through a prize roast. They drove slowly through the streets to avoid the revelers as they walked on both the sidewalk and the street stumbling around like toddlers. The van drove like it was going through a maze around the city. Lisa started to feel carsick. She was glad she did not have any alcohol before the drive. Lisa focused on the road ahead to try to stop the nausea. She saw a sign lit brightly that read St. Charles Hotel. *Thank God!* She felt relief as they pulled toward the front of the hotel. She got out carefully as to not make her nausea worse. She took a deep breath then followed Gabby into the hotel.

Lisa found herself surrounded by dozens of revelers dressed in their Mardi Gras' best. Men wore tuxedos and masks, topped off with a varied selection; from jester hats, to top hats, to crowns. Women wore formal floor-length gowns with opulent masks. Some wore gaudy jewelry and tiaras. Others wore fur stoles or feather boas. Lisa took in the scene of camp with wonder. She'd never seen such intricate costumes before; she loved it and felt exhilarated by the energy of the spectacle she had walked into. Lisa was so distracted looking at the different outfits, that she lost her family in the sea of masks as they took the stairs to the second level ballroom, where the music got louder and the people got drunker with every stair she ascended. When she arrived to the opulent ballroom, the smell of old bay, sounds of saxophones, glistening chandeliers, gold, purple, and green on every surface, and floating rounds of champagne coupes welcomed her. She scanned the room to try and spot her family. Just as Lisa was about to get her phone out of her purse to text Gabby, she caught the golden glow of Vivian's mask and dress. She spotted her family standing at their assigned table. She could tell that Joan was scanning the room looking for her, and Lisa quickly walked toward the table.

"Ah, there you are. We thought we lost you," Joan said as Lisa approached their table.

"I was for a slight second, luckily Vivian's glitter helped me identify everyone."

Holding her hands up in victory, Vivian confidently said, "Perfect! Mission accomplished, no one can lose me now."

As Lisa took her seat, she continued to survey the room. The jazz band was setting up while a DJ played a jazz/ party mix. The tables were large, they fit ten people each and had white table cloths with Mardi Gras colored skirts. They were decorated with large floral topiary centerpieces filled with roses, violets, tulips, carnations, and golden accents. The table tops were adorned with gold chargers and gold cutlery. Green, purple, and gold lights illuminated the walls. A giant sign that read "Happy Mardi Gras!" as well as the time duration from the app tracker was projected onto the wall behind the stage the band would play on. The wait staff hurried out baskets of bread and pitchers of water to the tables while the emcee for the night took the stage dressed in a white tuxedo and white top hat.

"Welcome to the tenth annual Armed Forces Ball!" he began, "The St. Charles Hotel throws a party every year to honor all our members in the military and their families. During this fun time, there is a silent auction happening tonight as well as a raffle for 2 free nights at the hotel. You can put in your bid and buy raffle tickets at the tables near the entrance. The proceeds benefit the Odysseus Foundation which helps pay for the medical bills of our wounded warriors. So, please buy some tickets. The buffets are now open with two rows of tables at either end of the room. They both have identical choices, so please feel free to start lining up at the table closest to yours. According to the app tracker, the parade is a good eighty minutes away, so enjoy your meal and the music. The balcony is open for when you want to watch the parade as well as bleachers downstairs, just show the security your wristband for access. Thank you for your service, and Happy Mardi Gras!" The trumpet roared as the band began playing.

"All right, here you go, Lisa! Here are your drink tickets for alcohol and your wristband. Soda and water are free, but for booze, you need a ticket or money," Joan said as she gave Lisa her two free booze tickets and a bright orange wristband.

"Where's mine?" Gabby asked.

"Aha," John said as he pointed to Gabby, "like Joan said, you don't need a ticket for soda or water."

"Fine," Gabby said before she took a sip of water.

"Let's go get our food," Steve said before standing up. Everyone else at the table followed his lead.

Lisa sat for a minute and secured her wristband before she got up and walked to the buffet table. The buffet was a creole feast fit for a king. One table was covered in chafing dishes filled with crawfish, shrimp, and mussels with potatoes, corn, and sausage, a traditional New Orleans boil. The table next to it had chicken jambalaya, red beans and rice, fried chicken, and a giant pot of gumbo. There were sides of potatoes, macaroni and cheese, salads, corn bread, dinner rolls, and a mixed vegetable dish. Lisa was impressed, she had never seen a spread like it before. The food smelled fresh, and the mountain of crawfish and crab still steamed from being boiled for hours warmed her up as she walked past it. She was hungry, and took a little bit of everything from the buffet.

After they returned to their table, everyone took off their masks so they could eat properly and enjoy their dinner.

"So, what did you do this week? Anything fun?" Steve asked John as he peeled a shrimp with his hands.

"I binge-watched seasons 2–4 of *Breaking Bad*. So, I'd say it was very productive," John said sarcastically as he pulled the head off a crawfish.

"Nice! I can't wait to be retired. I have around four shows on my list that I plan to watch when the kids are visiting my parents during the summer. But Viv here wants to go to Cabo, so we'll see if I'll be able to watch anything."

"Go to a place with good Wi-Fi and watch it by the pool."

"Yeah maybe, but I don't want her to get mad that I'm not unplugged enough."

John continued as he peeled a crawfish, "A lot of times for me, sitting and binge-watching a show is very relaxing."

"Exactly, same here."

"How's work going?"

"It's going all right. There is a horrible heroine epidemic that's causing a lot of traffic in the ER. It's a steady rotation of the same people. I feel like a Starbucks barista with their regular customers. The hospital also had to beef up security to make sure the junkies weren't stealing anything to feed their addiction. I just don't understand junkies."

Lisa observed and overheard her family's conversations but was too focused on peeling the crawfish to pay attention. She enjoyed the irony of the whole scene; she sat at a table with a combined eight university degrees including Steve, a physician. The ball had a strict formal dress code, yet everyone was peeling shrimp, crab, and crawfish with their bare hands.

"What's the significance of the parade tonight?" Lisa asked Vivian and Joan who sat to the right of her.

"Endymion is the god of the hunt, and known in the myth, as a very handsome king. The krewe that puts it on is known as a super krewe. The parade has over 3,000 riders, and it's the largest parade drawing the largest crowd. They end up in the superdome where the official ball is happening. They have televised concerts there too, it's a wild time. Their motto is 'throw until it hurts,'" Vivian explained to Lisa.

"Wow, that is awesome!" Lisa responded. She felt even more excited for tonight's parade after Vivian described the krewe and its origins. "I can't wait until it gets here. What about the colors? Do the Mardi Gras colors signify anything?"

"Yes, they do. Purple represents justice, green represents faith, and gold represents power."

"I love it!" Lisa responded.

She then continued to struggle with peeling her crawfish—the tiny red crustacean was winning the battle. It wasn't the first time she had crawfish, but she wasn't used to peeling them. When she visited family in Texas, they would have massive barbeques at her grandparents' house, which included crawfish though she never chose to eat them.

"You want some crawfish peelin' lessons?" Vivian asked Lisa.

"Yes, please! These suckers are a bit difficult for me."

Vivian grabbed a new crawfish to demo. Both Lisa and Gabby grabbed fresh crawfish, like two eager students learning a new lesson, they were ready to follow Vivian's crawfish peeling 101 lesson.

"First twist then pull off the head, but keep a firm hold on the lower end of the tail. Some people suck the juices out of the head, like the men over there but whatever." Vivian twisted the head of the crawfish and pulled it off while Lisa and Gabby mimicked her and did the exact same with theirs. "See how the meat has been partially exposed?" Vivian asked while pointing out the exposed meat of her crawfish. "Now peel off the rest of the shell body like so, and there is your freshly peeled crawfish!" Vivian said as she held up the perfectly peeled crawfish.

"Vivian has been peeling crawfish since she could eat solid foods," Joan commented before taking a bite of jambalaya.

"That's right, babe. Hey, now, don't let those drink tickets go to waste J, the bartender is giving them an Orleans pour," Vivian said as she began peeling another crawfish.

Quizzically, Lisa asked, "What's an Orleans pour?"

"A lot of booze," Vivian responded with a smile.

LOVE AND MARDI GRAS

The band started playing a very loud zydeco song. John started to sing along to the song, "Having a Party." "Come on, everybody, let's have a party, everybody, come on let's make a move."

Those who were done eating stood up to dance on the dance floor. It was the type of song that made everyone dance even while sitting in their seats. Lisa was enamored by the beauty and elegance of the ball. The next song the band started to play was, "The Way You Look Tonight." John and Joan got up to dance since this was their wedding dance song. Lisa smiled as she saw her aunt and uncle still in love and having fun. She longed to experience a love like theirs. She stared out at the dance floor and watched the couples dance. The view across the ballroom was no longer obstructed by John's giant jester hat. She could see every table and reveler in attendance. As she scanned the room, she noticed a man sitting at a table. He was staring at her.

They were separated by the dance floor, but they still they had a perfect view of each other. He stared at her and did not even pretend to look away when they locked eyes. Lisa felt the heat in her cheeks from blushing, she felt embarrassed. She tried to be coy and put on her mask. She hoped it would turn her invisible. *Oh lord*, she thought as she stared down at the table and tied the ribbon in the back of her head to fasten the mask. Her heart was racing, her whole body felt warm, she could feel the blood rush to her face. She looked up and noticed that he was still staring, and he smiled even bigger. He put on his mask too. It was black and only covered his eyes, like Zorro, which made his white smile pop out even more. Every time she looked in his direction, he was looking at her, at least she hoped that he was looking at her.

# CHAPTER 10

## *Endymion*

"25:13" WAS PROJECTED on the wall in bold purple numbers by the parade tracker app. Everyone was either dancing, mingling, or browsing the silent auction. The dessert and coffee bar were open, and the alcohol was ever flowing.

Lisa decided to walk around the ballroom and dance off her food coma. She spotted Joan standing at the auction table and walked toward where she was standing, curious to see what she was bidding on. It also provided the opportunity to steal glimpses in the direction of the handsome man she'd spotted across the room to keep tabs on what he was doing and who he was with.

"This event is perfectly timed, everything is planned to the T," Lisa said while she and Joan were browsing the silent auction tables.

"I guess it has to be since it was organized by military people," Joan responded. She picked up a pen and wrote in a bid for a wine basket.

"It all makes sense now," Lisa responded with a chuckle. The police cars began to chirp, signaling the parade was about to arrive.

"All right, y'all, you know what that sound means! Revelers, find a spot to watch on our balconies and street bleachers. The band is going to finish one last song before the parade arrives. The party has only just begun!" the emcee said over the microphone with 5:25 projected onto the wall.

Everyone went to their tables to grab coats and whatever else they needed to stand outside in the February night. Revelers topped off their drinks, women buttoned up their coats. Everyone got ready to assume position for the arrival of Endymion.

Lisa and her family walked onto the balcony just as the flambeaux were walking in front of the hotel. Lisa felt heat from the flambeaux fire on her face, it felt good in contrast to the chilly New Orleans winter evening. Following the flambeaux krewe were ten men dressed as knights in colors of Mardi Gras. A gold fleur-de-lis decorated their chests that glowed like armor. They rode on horses and tossed doubloons into the crowds. The drumming from the marching bands grew louder and louder until a wail of trumpets signaled that the parade had finally arrived. The first float was massive, the size of a small house. It was white with a giant gold crown and had a gold throne placed right in the middle. A man dressed as a king waved and threw beads to the revelers as the page boys waved to the crowd. The King of Endymion had arrived to get the party started.

A gold float that also had a throne atop it followed, it was the Queen of Endymion sitting on a throne as she waved to the crowd and tossed strands of beads. Her float also had a group of page boys that waved to the crowds. More members of the king's court followed; fifteen people dressed as knights followed the king's float wearing masks and outfits in the Mardi Gras colors, they rode confidently as they tossed more beads and Endymion doubloons into the crowds. Lisa felt like she was in an episode of *Game of Thrones*. A float of two younger-looking girls in ball gowns followed on a smaller float the size of an RV; they threw beads and wore red ball gowns and opulent tiaras. They were princesses of the parade. Lisa was infatuated because it made her own high school homecoming court experience look like a children's play compared to this marvelous production.

A Marine Corps citadel marching band playing, "When the Saints Come Marching In", followed the knights and royal court. Every reveler stood to their feet out of respect and clapped. When the marching band arrived in front of the hotel, the military revelers yelled, "OORAH." Lisa stood on the balcony with her family. She felt like royalty as she looked out at the hundreds of people lining the streets below. Following the citadel, was a double-decker float in the shape of a dragon, its mouth was open, a confetti cannon blew orange confetti, lights, and smoke out of its mouth like fire. Riders were scattered along the back of the dragon dressed as knights; they threw beads in every direction at the crowds. One rider aimed to throw beads at Lisa, but the beads were thrown so high over Lisa's head that a few ended up stuck on the ledge of a windowsill two stories above the balcony she was standing on. Lisa ducked, covered, dashed, and passed the beads that were being thrown at her in droves.

After thirty minutes of the parade, floats, and catching beads, Lisa's feet began to hurt. She felt the balls of her feet begin to burn. *Dammit!* She cursed herself for not bringing a pair of flats to change into, and the night was too cold to go barefoot. She glanced in the empty ballroom and noticed that there was a first aid box hanging on the wall. *Band-Aids!* she thought to herself as she hurried inside. She grabbed some Band-Aids from the first aid kit and took a seat at the table.

"Ouch, ouch," she said as she took off her heels.

Her toes were red and throbbed as if they were saying *thank you* to her for giving them a rest. She sat for a few minutes with her feet elevated on a chair. She could see her family on the balcony dancing and enjoying the parade. She smiled as she watched them. She sat and reflected at how drastic her week had been. Just two days ago, she was confused, alone, and consumed with depression. Now she was at a ball in New Orleans having the time of her life with her family and new friends. She was starting to feel loved and accepted instead of lonely and rejected. *Oh my god, that feels good,* Lisa thought as she sat at the table with her feet perched up on a chair. She began to put Band-Aids on the blistering parts of her toes and feet. After a few more minutes of rest, she put her heels back on. But before she went back outside to the balcony, she took a detour to the dessert table.

The table was covered with a giant king cake that was already halfway eaten. On each side of the giant cake were tall multitiered stands of cupcakes, macarons, and cake pops. The desserts were intricately decorated in gold, purple, and green. There was a coffee table next to the dessert table covered with beignets. She felt like she was at one of the famous Marie Antoinette parties at the Palace of Versailles. As Lisa reached for a slice of king cake, she heard a voice from her side. It was a man's voice. The voice sounded smooth and seemingly nice.

"That's got to be the biggest king cake in all of New Orleans."

Lisa turned to see who it was speaking to her. It was the guy she spotted earlier from across the room. He was still wearing his mask. He was taller than she expected. His perfectly styled dark brown hair and brown eyes made him seem like he was an actor from the '50s, a Don Draper type that would've looked perfect playing opposite Grace Kelly. He was a man of mystery, a mystery that she wanted to solve.

"Yeah, it's pretty big, you think they entered it into the Guinness records or something?" *Gosh,* Lisa said to herself, *think of something cooler to say.*

"Well, if they did, I hope the judges already came since it's nearly gone. That would be cool though, it would be a shame to go unnoticed for this hard work," Mike said as he gestured to the cake as if he were presenting it.

"Maybe the person who made it doesn't want recognition. Maybe they just wanted to make it for the pure love of it."

"Ahh, a true artist."

"Yeah, I guess."

"No, I meant you. I'm Mike," he said as he held out his hand to shake Lisa's.

"Lisa," she responded as she shook his hand. Lisa felt an immediate connection as she stared into Mike's eyes.

"So, am I right?" Mike asked.

Lisa stood staring at him with a grin, mesmerized by his smile. She was curious like a detective trying to profile her suspect. "Wait, what?" she responded.

"An artist, are you an artist?"

"Hardly, I paint for fun. I love photography and a good water-color. But I wouldn't classify myself as an artist."

"Nonsense, everyone is an artist in one way or another."

Playfully, she asked, "So, what's your art then?"

"Music, I love to play my guitar."

"Very nice," Lisa responded as she put a cake pop on her plate. Mike grabbed a plate and did the same.

*Pop!* The bartender had opened a champagne bottle for a reveler wanting a glass.

"The party never stops!" Mike commented.

She smiled and turned to Mike. "I love that pop, it's such a happy sound."

He smiled. "Who are you here with? Family? Friends? Husband? Boyfriend?"

"I'm visiting with my family. I'm here with my aunt, uncle, and cousin."

"So, you're not the one in the military? And no boyfriend?" Mike further inquired.

Lisa smiled and replied, "No, I'm a civilian and no boyfriend, happily single over here."

"Ahh, that's nice," Mike said as they both walked to a table.

"Who are you here with? Are you in the military?" Lisa inquired.

"I'm here with my friends, and we're all in the Air Force."

"Awesome, I love the Air Force. My dad is retired from the Air Force. What do you do in the Air Force?" she asked before taking a bite of a cake pop.

"Mechanical engineer. But I'm in law school at Tulane. So, how do you like New Orleans?"

"How do you know I'm not from here?" She was surprised that he knew she was from California.

"The California accent is a clue. I grew up near Seattle, so I can spot a fellow west coaster."

"I love it here! It's like a small European city but in America. It has so much life, energy, and character."

"Ahh, I was correct, you're Californian. It's beautiful there too."

"Yeah, it's beautiful. I feel like it's one of the most historical places in the world. Even though it's a young state compared to places like London and Rome, the entertainment, innovations, an architecture give it such a unique history. You can be in one building that is deemed a historical treasure from the 1800s. Or you can be in Pasadena, walking down the same street Marilyn Monroe once walked, while also walking near the NASA Jet Propulsion lab, where innovations in science and technology are developed. It's sort of like a place for everyone, anyone can find a place to identify and fall in love with."

"Yeah, I can see that. How long are you visiting here for?"

"I'll be here until Monday." Lisa liked how interested he seemed to be in her. She felt pursued and wanted, which made her feel good. She had butterflies in her stomach whenever he asked her a question.

"Great! Want to check out the parade?" he asked.

"Sure!"

*Who is this guy!* Lisa thought. She was excited but nervous, she tried to remain poised. As they walked to the balcony, they dodged beads that flew like rockets through the air. They walked to the spot where Lisa's family was. John and Steve had already caught so many beads their necks were almost completely covered. Joan only kept the beads she liked. Vivian only kept the gold and white ones to match her outfit.

"Hey, now, where are all your beads?" John drunkenly asked Lisa.

"I was taking a break, hanging out in the ballroom. This is Mike, he's in the Air Force," Lisa said as she introduced Mike to John.

"It is very nice to meet you," John said while shaking Mike's hand.

"Nice meeting you too, sir," Mike responded while shaking John's and Steve's hands.

"So, what do you do?" Steve asked Mike.

"I'm a mechanical engineer in the Air Force, but I'm in law school right now. What about you? Lisa said you are all in the Coast Guard."

"I'm a retired drill sergeant," John responded.

"Oh wow, awesome," Mike responded.

Steve laughed. "Look at the fear in his eyes! You must've gotten broke down bad from your drill sergeant."

"Our beautiful wives over there are both officers," John said as he motioned to where Vivian and Joan stood before taking a sip of his beer. Vivian noticed the men pointing to them, she and Joan walked to where the guys were standing since she thought their husbands needed them.

"What are you two plotting?" Vivian inquired.

"Nothing, this is our new friend, Mike," Steve said as he patted Mike's shoulder.

"Nice to meet you, Mike," Vivian said as she extended her hand to shake his.

"I'm Joan," Joan said as she shook Mike's hand.

"They're talking about boot camp stuff," Lisa filled Vivian in.

"Ahh, fun times. What branch are you in?" Vivian asked Mike.

"Air Force."

"Awesome! Where are you stationed?" Vivian asked.

"I'm at the New Orleans air base right now. I'm also in law school."

"How much longer do you have?" Vivian asked quickly.

"One more year, then who knows where I'll be," Mike responded.

"Yeah, we all know how that is," John chimed in. "We just got sent to Elizabeth City for Joan's current tour."

"You're not here by yourself, are you?" Vivian asked Mike concernedly.

"No, my friends are around here somewhere."

"HEADS UP!" John hollered while a float throwing beads came into their section. Beads were flying everywhere.

Mike caught a handful and put them on Lisa. "Here, you need more," he said as he put them gently around her neck.

"Here's one for you," she said as she put the string of beads with an Endymion medallion on him. She brushed his lapel which had an Air Force pin placed perfectly in the boutonniere. She could feel his muscle-defined chest and blushed a little.

As the float passed, there was a block before the next marching band approached. "I see my friends," Mike said to Lisa as he pointed them out to her. Lisa and Mike both looked down from the balcony onto the street view, and he noticed his friends staring up at them, one of them motioned for Mike to come down.

"I think I should go back down there and see what's up," Mike said to Lisa.

She smiled. "Okay, see you later."

"Yes, the night is young."

"Indeed it is," she responded. They stared at each other as he walked away toward the elevator. Lisa looked around the balcony and saw Gabby standing alone. Lisa walked toward her to stand next to her.

"Where'd your friend go?" Gabby asked as she moved over to make room for Lisa to join her at the front of the balcony, it was the perfect spot to see and be seen.

"His friends are somewhere down there, so he went to hang out with them."

A float that was decorated to look like a jungle passed by, throwing plenty of green beads. After a few minutes, there was a break in the parade. Lisa was safe to scan her surroundings. She spotted Mike below, drinking a beer and talking to his friends.

She was still trying to gauge who he was there with. He was talking to a few girls, but his body language didn't communicate that they were friends. A drill team and marching band walked in front of the hotel playing "Crazy in Love" by Beyoncé loudly. She had never heard the trumpets play the hook to the song in person, and her heart raced to the sound and beat; she loved the song and loved it even more played by a marching band. Gabby and Lisa danced, cheered, and marveled at the drill team. Once the marching band passed, Lisa looked down toward Mike. He was staring up at her, smiling, he clearly watched as her and Gabby gyrated to the song. Mike and Lisa made eye contact. She smiled and gave him a modest nod and an ever-so-coolly wave even though she wanted to wave erratically. He smiled, nodded, and lifted his beer. One of Mike's friends broke their gaze and put a shot glass in Mike's hand. Lisa watched as the three men and one woman took a shot, the other girls he had been talking to were not in the shot circle, which gave Lisa hope that he was there and he was single.

"Okay, I need a drink," Lisa said to Gabby as she walked back inside to grab a glass of champagne from the bar.

"Here you go," Vivian said as she handed out champagne coupes to her and Joan. "Cheers to us, ladies!"

"Cheers!" Lisa and Joan responded as they clinked their plastic coupes together and took a swig of champagne.

The parade rolled on for another hour. Massive and ornate floats the size of buildings rolled down the street, all decorated in garden themes, playing music and shooting out cannon balls of confetti. Marching bands and drill teams from all over Louisiana kept the party filled with music while the drum lines kept hearts racing. Dozens of beads and other types of throws, such as cups, reusable bags, doubloons, stuffed animals, and masks, were thrown from the floats as if there was a never-ending supply. Just as Lisa thought a float was out of throws, they kept bringing out bags from behind the riders and threw more and more. Everyone drank, laughed, dodged throws, caught throws, and enjoyed the parade. Lisa stared at the massive amounts of beads that piled up on the balcony that formed little mounds like sparkly anthills. She felt happy and exhilarated; she had never experienced a night like this before. It was in the words of one of her favorite novels, a moveable feast. It felt like prom or some other fun milestone type of night that felt special and unique. It was a glamourous ball, a crazy party, and a parade all in one night.

Once the parade ended, the masses scattered in every direction across the city to continue to party. But luckily for Lisa, the party continued at the St. Charles Hotel. The music fluctuated from modern dance to classic New Orleans jazz; people were drunk and happy. After about thirty minutes of being with each of their respective groups, Lisa was drunk enough but not yet sloppy enough to approach Mike.

"Hey, hey," Lisa said as she approached Mike who was standing along the perimeter of the dance floor with his friends.

"Hey! How's it goin'?" he said with a smile.

"Great! Why aren't you dancing?"

"Would you like to dance?" Mike asked while he held out his hand to Lisa.

"I'm not really sure how to dance to this." The band was playing a traditional zydeco medley.

"Me neither, just go with it."

Lisa nodded 'yes' while accepting Mike's hand. He led her onto the dance floor. They danced and laughed and looked ridiculous since they were not coordinated with each other. They danced a waltz combined with a two-step to a jazzy song; just as they got a hold of the rhythm, the song ended.

"Oh man, that was fun!" Lisa said as she fanned herself.

"Yeah, it was a struggle at first, but we figured it out. Shall we keep going?" Mike asked while holding out his hand in a way that signaled he was going to twirl her around.

"Sure!" Lisa said as she twirled. They danced to one more song.

"Where'd you learn to dance so well?" Lisa asked. She enjoyed dancing with him, he was a good leader, which she appreciated in a dance partner.

"I got the beat."

"Yes, I can tell!"

"I had to take cotillion as a kid. My grandmother was Austrian, so she made sure everyone in the family knew how to waltz. But I have no idea how to dance zydeco, so I just go for it. Life's too short to be worrying about what others are thinking about you. What about you? You're a pretty good dancer as well, did you ever take any lessons?"

"Do quinceañera waltz practices count? My friends and I like to go out dancing too, salsa or line dancing, whatever our mood is."

"Oh cool, salsa dancing. I've never been, you'll have to teach me one day."

She teased. "Yeah, if you're lucky."

They continued to dance and laugh in a graceless circle of delight. The lights moved to the music while the sparkle of the beads on the revelers' necks provided extra luminance. The dance floor was packed with happy drunk people covered in beads and whatever wearable throws they caught.

The emcee stepped on stage and announced, "All right, y'all, the band is going to take a quick break, enjoy the DJ for a little bit." A free dance song came on, and Lisa and Mike were approached by Mike's friends, three guys wearing beads and holding beers.

"Lisa, these are my friends," he said as he lightly held her arm and motioned to his friends respectfully and full of hospitality. "Miles, though we call him Moose, Joe, and Ric." Lisa had recognized them. They were the same men she had noticed him sharing a table with.

"How do you do?" she said as the shook all their hands. They all smiled at each other and danced like old friends.

A woman approached their group holding a champagne coupe. "There she is. Lisa, this is Melissa, Joe's wife," Mike said as he introduced Lisa to Melissa.

"Nice meeting you," Lisa said as she extended her hand to shake Melissa's.

"You as well," Melissa responded, smiling big and dancing next to Joe. The music was too loud to have any other conversations, they all danced around each other.

"Hey, Mikey!" John said as he and Joan came over to dance along with them.

Mike shook John's hand. Both Lisa's family and friends became introduced, acquainted, and integrated with Mike's friends as the DJ played some New Orleans styled dance and hip-hop songs while the band took a quick break.

The time was 1:45 AM. The emcee, who was flanked in beads and sweating from dancing, jumped on stage when there was a break in the music to give an announcement. "All right, y'all, last call and last song, let's make this one count." The jazz band was back on stage and started playing the classic New Orleans song "Do Whatcha Wanna." Everyone who knew the lyrics or at least thought they knew the lyrics sang along to the lively song as they danced to every note.

The brass band stood up from their chairs and walked into the crowd, creating a second line in the party while they continued to play their hearts out for ten more minutes past the end point of the song. The partygoers danced and sang along to every note and followed the band like a mini parade. Lisa felt sweaty, and her heart pumped like she was in her kickboxing class. When the song officially ended, the dance floor erupted in an applause. The lead trumpet player jumped back on stage took the microphone to make an announcement, "Thank you! We are the Jazz Kings! Y'all get home safe now, and Happy Mardi Gras!"

The ballroom chandelier started to gradually get brighter as someone was raising the dimmer switch. The strobe lights and lasers were turned off, the party at the St. Charles Hotel was over.

"What are you doing after this?" Mike asked Lisa.

The time was 2:00 AM. She glanced over at her family who were walking back to their table. They walked slowly and looked exhausted. They were gathering their things and throws and started to put on their coats.

"Just go back to our hotel, I guess," Lisa replied.

"Want to come out with us?" Moose asked.

Though she wanted to answer "yes" with every bone in her body to spend more time with Mike, she recognized her own exhaustion. "I'm good," she replied. "I'm tired and want to spend time with my family."

"Will you be here for the parades tomorrow?" Mike asked.

"Yeah, I think so."

"Can I get your number? You know just in case you go somewhere else," Mike said as he got out his phone and handed it to her.

Excited, she said, "Yes." Lisa had a huge smile as she entered her number into his phone.

Mike called it immediately to make sure that she didn't accidently put in the wrong number, but her phone was in her purse at the table.

"It went to voice mail. Hey, Lisa, this is Mike, it was cool meeting you, and now you have my number, talk to you later. You have a voice message now."

"Cool, thanks for letting me know."

"Well, have a good night, Miss...?" Mike said in an asking way to learn her last name.

85

"Perez."

"Have a good night, Miss Perez."

"You have a good night as well, Mr. Mike...?"

"Mike Martin."

"Have a good night, Mr. Martin," Lisa said then turned to walk to her family.

Mike walked the opposite direction to his table across the dance floor from hers to where his friends were gathering up their belongings.

"You two seemed to have hit it off," Joan said to Lisa.

"Yeah, he's cool. Hopefully we'll see each other tomorrow during Bacchus. We'll be coming back here to watch it, right?"

"Yeah, but there's no ball, just casual tailgating, and the parades start at 2:00 PM, so we'll just be hanging out all day."

As Lisa and her family got to the lobby of the St. Charles Hotel, the cleaning crews and street sweepers had taken over the parade route, making it hard to cross the street.

"How are we going to get back, Dad?" Gabby asked John in a tired voice.

"We can cross over there, that will put us by touchdown Jesus and spit us back onto Canal Street," John said as he pointed in the direction they needed to go toward the famed city statue known as touchdown Jesus. Lisa walked, quickly and carefully. She was drunk enough that her high heels didn't hurt her feet anymore but sober enough to navigate the cracks and potholes safely. The air was cold, but the mask was like a shield and protected Lisa's nose and eyes from the cold air. The beads acted like a scarf, which kept her warm and clicked and clacked with every step she made.

"What's touchdown Jesus?" Lisa asked Joan who was walking beside her.

"In the back of St. Louis Cathedral, that big white church," Joan said as she pointed to St Louis Cathedral they were walking toward, "there's a statue of Jesus holding his hands up in the air. At night, a spotlight shines on him, casting his shadow on the building that looks like a goalpost, and his arms are up like a football referee calling a touchdown," Joan said as they turned the corner, and the statue came into Lisa's eye view. Joan pointed out the statue that looked small, casting a large shadow on the back of church.

"That's so funny! Oh my goodness, it really does look like a ref calling a touchdown," Lisa commented. She loved learning the local stories and little idiosyncrasies of a new city that was only learnt when traveling and becoming integrated with locals. Her family stopped to look at the famed statue to take in the splendor of a delightful unintended consequence of a simple statue of Jesus.

"People use it as a geographical marker too. If someone is lost, you can always find out where they are in relation to touchdown Jesus. Or if you're meeting someone, you can say to meet in front of touchdown Jesus, and people will know exactly what you are talking about," Vivian explained.

Lisa and her family continued to walk toward Canal Street, and before she knew it, they arrived to The Roosevelt Hotel. She was amazed that John's drunken navigation skills got her family and their friends safely to their hotel. The lobby of the hotel was still buzzing with a lively party at the Sazerac bar. Vivian and Steve diverted to the valet counter to drive home. Lisa and Gabby said good night to them and quickly headed up to their room while Joan and John stayed to see them off. Lisa and Gabby both took off their shoes in the elevator.

"Oh my god, that feels good," Gabby said as she took off her heels.

"Yes, I can't believe I didn't bring flats, I don't know what I was thinking."

"I took mine off at the ball, I couldn't take it," Gabby said. "But that walk officially did my toes in."

They both walked quickly barefoot down the hall of a luxury hotel to their room and quickly put their beads into the dedicated bead drawer of the dresser.

"You can use the bathroom first," Lisa said to Gabby.

"Thank you!" Gabby said in earnest as she grabbed her pajamas and headed into the bathroom.

Lisa quickly took off her dress and put on her pajamas while no one was in the room. She took out a makeup wipe and started to wipe off her face. She looked at her phone and remembered that he left her a voice mail. She could feel the blood rush to her cheeks; even hearing his voice made her blush. She texted him back to let him know that the message was received: Got your message. Good night!

"Nite." She blushed and the butterflies fluttered when he texted back promptly.

*Was this the rebound? Was this the guy Joan had predicted?* she mused and thought about Mike's smile, and holding his hands as they danced. She was happy, she was excited, but she was spent. She looked forward to laying down and sleeping. She couldn't wait to see him again.

# CHAPTER 11

## The Court of Two Sisters

LISA FELT THE glow of the light on her closed eyes as the morning sun peeked through the crack of the curtains as she lay in bed during the Sunday morning hours. Joan was the first one awake enough to get out of bed and make efforts to begin the day. Lisa got up around 9:00 AM, the same time her family started to wake up. They all sat in a groggy silence as they slowly woke up. Lisa laid in bed, reflecting on the previous night at the ball. The entire night felt like a dream, with the costumes, food, fantastic music, parade theatrics, dancing, and Mike.

Mike Martin, the man in the mask who looked at her like she was the only woman in the room. But the soreness of her legs assured her that it was not a dream. She felt more open than she usually was and was receptive to Mike and his friends instead of closed off. She was proud of herself and the evening of being an extrovert. She gave credit to the mask for her confidence, it certainly brought a different side of her out that she would not have been able to be without the comfort and the barrier of the playful mask. Lisa still felt giddy when she thought about Mike. She tried to imagine his face, the curve of his jaw, and his perfect Oscar-winning smile. But she could mainly remember how he made her feel. He made her feel valued and seen.

Not disposable like how her ex made her feel. Last night was everything she had hoped for, and more than what she expected.

John was hungover and didn't physically get out of bed until 10:00 AM. He stacked the pillows to prop him up so that he could watch television as the women took their turns using the bathroom and get ready for the day. When it was his turn to use the bathroom, John got out of bed and walked slowly like a zombie to peer out the window. His body cracked as he walked. "Gah!" he shouted as if he pulled a muscle. He looked tired, spent, and hungover. "Lovely morning," John commented as he looked out of the window and stared at the clear blue sky. He grabbed the clothes that he would wear for the day and walked slowly to the bathroom. He was the last one left to shower and get ready. The rest of the ladies were finishing up with their hair and makeup in the main room as they watched the *History of Mardi Gras* on the local PBS station.

"Is he alive? I haven't heard the shower," Gabby commented as she was putting on her shoes.

Joan made a curious look with her face as she furrowed her brow and waked over to the bathroom door. "Baby, are you comin' or are you sick?" Joan asked John through the bathroom door.

The shower turned on. Over the noise of the shower, John hollered, "Naw, I'm fine. I'll get ready real quick. Y'all start heading toward the restaurant. I'll follow shortly."

"All right," Joan said. Lisa, Gabby, and Joan gathered their purses, put on their coats, and made their way out of the room.

"I bet he's been waiting all morning for us to leave so he can stink up the bathroom," Joan said as they were in the elevator going down to the lobby. "See, Lisa, this is what you have to look forward to with marriage."

"Ewe," Lisa responded as she shook her head.

The lobby was calm. The guests and workers moved about the building in slow motion. Everyone was tired, nursing a hangover, or a combination of both. The ladies walked through the lobby doors out onto the sidewalk into the cold winter morning air of New Orleans. Lisa buttoned up her coat. Given that it was sunny and clear, she thought that it looked warmer than it really was. They crossed Canal Street and entered the French Quarter, jumping over puddles that remained from the residents who used garden hoses to wash the fronts of their houses and storefronts. The air smelled fresh, the breeze on Lisa's nose helped to wake her up.

"Never attempt to walk through a puddle here. The potholes can be super deep. Cars have even been known to get stuck in them," Joan said as they walked and dodged puddles along Royal Street.

Lisa had been looking forward to this brunch ever since she landed at the airport.

"Good morning, welcome to The Court of Two Sisters," the hostess said with a smile.

"Good morning, I have a reservation for four, the name is Perez," Joan said as she approached the hostess desk in the foyer of the restaurant.

"Okay, let me see," the hostess said as she scanned through the hostess stand registration table. "Yes, here you are, right this way, ma'am." They followed her past iron gates through a dark brick-lined hallway. "Now, since it's a bit cold this morning, would you like to sit in the dining room or in the atrium?"

"Atrium," Gabby quickly responded.

"Great, follow me, please," the hostess said as she escorted them into a giant white room surrounded by windows that let every ray of light in.

The room glowed, and the silver cutlery sparkled atop the crisp white tablecloths. The doors opened to the lush courtyard that contained a large fountain that glistened in the sunlight like it knew people were watching it. The restaurant felt completely isolated from the chaos of Mardi Gras that was just outside its front heavy doors. The atmosphere was peaceful, and the air smelled sweet. Lisa's ears perked when she heard the jazz band was playing "La Vie en Rose."

"I love this song!" Lisa exclaimed. Their table was located across the room from the jazz band that was centrally located so that they could be heard at every seat in the restaurant.

"The beverage menu is on the table. Your server will be here shortly. Help yourself to the buffet when you are ready," the hostess said while the ladies got settled into their table.

"There he is," Lisa said as she saw John walking quickly toward them, still wearing his sunglasses. He looked like a celebrity trying to remain incognito.

"Hey, babe," John said as he kissed Joan on the cheek before taking his seat. He sat calmly and quietly.

"Did the shower fix your hangover?" Lisa asked.

"Nope, I need coffee," John responded as he took off his sunglasses and laid them on the table; he rubbed his eyes to acclimate his vision to the bright room. In less than a minute, the server came to the table ready to take drink orders.

"Good morning, welcome to The Court of Two Sisters. May I take your beverage orders before you go to the buffet tables?"

"Good morning, sir, I will take a Bloody Mary, please."

"I'll take a coffee," Joan said.

"I'll get coffee as well," said Gabby.

"Same here," said Lisa.

Joan chimed in, "Oh, and water's all around too, please,"

"Great, I'll bring those out for y'all," the server responded.

"Bloody Mary? Thought you needed coffee," Lisa asked John.

"Nothing fixes a hangover more effectively than a Bloody Mary. It's in the bible."

They all gave a little laughter and perked up when they got the whiff of fresh bacon being brought to the buffet.

"Okay, time for food, I'm following that guy," Gabby said as she stood up and walked to the buffet.

"Me too," Lisa said as she followed Gabby.

Joan stayed back and visited with John for a little bit before they got up to get food. Lisa observed them from the buffet line. She took mental notes of how Joan interacted with John. She wanted to learn her strategy for how she interacted with her husband and carry those lessons into her next relationship. But the moment of observations made Lisa feel melancholic. She wanted someone to have special moments with again. Her ex had accused her of being emotionally disconnected and disinterested. There are moments she'll see things happening in successful relationships and wished she could go back and do those little things with her ex. But instead, all she could do was emulate what she sees and wait for the next relationship.

The two large buffet tables were covered with biscuits, omelet station, pancakes, waffles, crawfish etouffee, shrimp cocktail, turtle soup, fruit, bacon and sausage. There was a window that led to the kitchen with two chefs working diligently, pulling poached eggs out of steaming pots. It was an eggs Benedict station, which Lisa immediately made a beeline toward. Lisa was in heaven. Brunch was Lisa's favorite meal, and a creole brunch buffet felt to her like a religious experience. She piled food onto her plate like it was her last meal. After her plate was filled, she quickly made her way back to the table. She was excited to try these new creole flavors that were rarely found in California. Lisa and her family ate in peace, they didn't speak much, they all enjoyed the food and the jazz band that created the perfect soundtrack to the lovely brunch.

"So, what do you think of Mardi Gras so far, Lis? Gabs?" John asked.

"I'm ruined when it comes to parades now. I'll never be able to go to one anywhere else and be just as involved. That's one of the cool parts I've noticed about these parades, you're not just watching, with the beads and things they throw, you're taking part in it as well," Lisa responded.

"Yeah, it's different. It's an interactive experience for sure. I love it. I want to come back as many times as I can," Gabby said.

"Seriously, nothing in California can compare to these parades and parties. Last night, everyone was drunk, but they were happy. I haven't seen any fights or any violence, and people are super drunk. This restaurant with this French decor and the beautiful lush garden views is just stunning. It's one of the most beautiful restaurants I've ever been in," Lisa said before taking a bite of bacon.

"Yeah, this is one of my favorite restaurants in the world. It's where the governors, politicians, and high society used to hang out at when the city was considered part of France. People have been coming here to eat and have their afternoon tea for centuries. People can also rent out the courtyard for parties. I've been to a few bridal and baby showers here."

"What are we going to do today?" Gabby asked.

Joan held her coffee in both hands and responded, "Well, I was thinking since it's our last full day here, we can do a little shopping on Royal Street. Then go back to the hotel and relax before heading to the St. Charles for our last night of parading. Vivian and Steve are going to join us all day at the parades."

"Sounds good," Lisa said while cutting a piece of sausage. She had forgotten about her ex and Mike. The only thing that mattered to her at that moment was her food.

"My goodness, that piano sounds amazing!" Joan commented.

They all took a minute to watch the band as the pianist lead the group in playing "Blue Drag." The classic French song made Lisa feel like she was in Europe, where the atmosphere is as important as the food, where servers leave you alone to enjoy every aspect of the meal, and where every table of a restaurant is meant for you to sit, relax, and escape. After they finished their food and coffees, John paid the bill, and they all got up to leave the restaurant. As she followed her family toward the foyer, Lisa turned back and took in one last look out at the bright atrium and courtyard, before following her family through the dark foyer to the street.

As they stood on the sidewalk outside of the entrance to The Court of Two Sisters, John leaned into Joan, gave her a kiss on the cheek, and said, "Welp, see you later!"

"Dad, you're not coming?"

"Shopping? No. Y'all have fun. Text me when you're headed back," he said as he walked toward Canal Street. He turned and waved and shouted "Love y'all" before disappearing in the crowd of people that were walking along Royal Street in and out of shops.

"All right, let's go this way. I remember there is a garden shop I wanted to check out," Joan said as she motioned in the opposite direction. The ladies walked shop to shop, making a maze around the French Quarter. They indulged in praline samples at every candy shop they passed. Joan pointed out special sights and streets, like a tour guide. As they walked around the quarter, Joan pointed out a large sign atop a restaurant that said Antoine's.

"Antoine's has a special ballroom where they have a king cake party in every year on Twelfth Night to kick off the Mardi Gras season. In fact, it's considered a party foul to eat king cake before January 6th. That's when Mardi Gras really starts and parades start rolling through the streets," Joan educated Lisa and Gabby like a tour guide.

"Have you ever been to the Antoine's party?" Lisa asked.

"No, I wish. It's very exclusive to the restaurateur set here and invite only," Joan replied.

Lisa felt her phone vibrate in her pocket. She took out her phone to check her messages, it was from a number she didn't recognize. Her heart started to beat faster; she felt the blood rushing to her cheeks when she saw Mike's name. She felt giddy and excited like she was a teenager again.

MIKE: Hey, it's Mike!
LISA. Buenos días! how are you?

Lisa felt her cheeks get warm, she was blushing and smiling. She could barely contain her happiness to receive a text message from him. She tried to keep him on read, but she couldn't help but respond right away.

MIKE: Fine, I woke up not too long ago. Just fixing to get ready and grab some food. What are you up to today?
LISA: Nothing much, we just got done with brunch. Now we're shopping. Later we're heading back to the St. Charles to watch the parades.
MIKE: Okay, awesome, I'll see you there then.
LISA: Yep, see you there.

Lisa was happy that Mike messaged her. But she was nervous to see him again. Happy because he was obviously interested in her. Nervous because there was no mask, no glitz, no glamour to hide under, tonight she would be herself. Lisa bought a fleur-de-lis necklace she saw at one of the shops and put it on immediately. She always liked the fleur-de-lis, meaning "flower of light." She was always interested in the connection it had historically, and the spiritual meaning as well. Aesthetically, she thought it looked beautiful. She had always admired Joan's fleur-de-lis necklace that she wore all the time and wanted one for herself. This one was perfect; it was covered in rhinestones and laid perfectly in a silver chain. They walked next door to another shop that primarily sold clothes and novelty shirts. Lisa saw a rack with purple tank tops that piqued her interest. The shirt had a French phrase in gold lettering on the front.

"What does *laissez les bons temps rouler* mean?" Lisa asked Joan as she held up the shirt and attempted to read the French words.

"*Laissez les bons temps rouler*," Joan said in perfect French, "it means let the good times roll, like the parades rolling. It's a typical saying around here. I like that shirt. I may buy it."

"I want one too!" Gabby exclaimed.

"I'll get it for all three of us. I've always loved this saying," Joan said as she picked out a small for Gabby and two mediums for her and Lisa.

"Thanks, Aunt Joan!"

"Yeah, thanks, Joan."

They continued to browse the store for a few minutes before checking out at the register. Lisa purchased a magnet for Allison, pralines for her coworkers and parents, and a few other small things to fit in her carry-on. They exited the store and continued to walk around the French Quarter. They tried to stay on the sidewalk, beneath the awnings, to avoid getting hit by flying beads.

"Can we go in the voodoo shop?" Gabby asked Joan.

"Sure."

The shop was illuminated with a purple light. Lisa felt calm and peace as soon as she walked into the shop. The shop smelled of incense, sage, and various dried herbs. The herbs were wrapped in special linen bags that had labels on them, signifying what they were used for. One bag signified money and wealth, another was for love. There were voodoo dolls, trinkets, candles, and New Orleans artifacts everywhere. It was a gift shop for the occult and those who came to the city for the dark history. They had clearly fake and manufactured figurine voodoo dolls as well as real ones to be made and modified. A sign was posted near the voodoo dolls that read *Ask Any Employee to Wake Up Your Doll*. Lisa was enamored by the shop. *Allison would love it here*, she thought. She saw a string of glass beads and picked them up.

"Lisa, no!" Gabby said concerningly.

"What?"

"You just took beads from Marie."

Lisa looked back at where the beads came from and noticed there was picture of Marie Laveau. Lisa had accidently taken beads from the shrine dedicated to Marie Laveau with candles, incense, jewelry, money, etc. Any offering someone wanted to give to the Voodoo Queen of New Orleans was left at the altar.

"Oh crap," Lisa said when she noticed what she had done.

"Here, put more beads on her shrine," Gabby said as she took off a string from her neck and handed it to Lisa.

"Umm okay. Sorry, Madame Marie," Lisa said as she put the string of beads on her shrine then quickly walked away to find Joan. Lisa and Gabby located Joan in the back of the store who was looking at a wall of stickers.

Joan turned to Lisa and said laughing, "When I was going through my divorce, a friend of mine gave me a sticker from here that has a picture of a voodoo doll on it with needles sticking into it, and it says 'Always remember to check in with your ex.'"

"Hmm, maybe I should get a doll for checking in with Matt. I'm sure there's still some strands of his hair on one of my brushes he would use," Lisa said jokingly.

She went through a small moment of wanting revenge after she found out that her ex was cheating on her. But between having to move to a new apartment and her friends offering to distract her, she never acted on any of her revenge ideas. Luckily, she decided to let karma take care of him and walk away with her dignity.

Gabby bought a voodoo doll for herself and a friend. Lisa looked around at the herbs wall when a woman who worked at the store approached her with a giant smile on her face. It was not an inquiring-customer-service smile, but a telling smile, like she had a secret to share.

"Do you have any questions?" the woman asked Lisa, staring intently into her eyes and examining her face as if she was reading her.

"No, thanks, I'm just looking," Lisa politely responded.

"Not about the candles. Do you have any questions?" the woman asked Lisa again, her face looking intent as if she was hoping Lisa would ask a question.

"I'm okay."

"Okay, great. Just so you know, you are beautiful. You're more beautiful than you think you are. Always know that. Always know you have beauty within. Always know that no one, no man or any-one, can take that away. All you have to do is focus on the rose inside of you," the woman said to Lisa with conviction and intensity. She stared into Lisa's eyes like she was in a trance, like she was a coach trying to tell their star player the game winning play. Lisa felt a chill down her spine as she received the woman's message and felt imme-diately grateful and flattered by this woman's read.

"Thank you, I appreciate that," Lisa said before she walked quickly outside to where Joan and Gabby were waiting. She won-dered if her low self-esteem was noticeable to non-mediums. She felt assured there was a little glimmer of herself that remained, which gave her a confidence boost.

"Did you buy anything?" Gabby asked Lisa as they continued to walk around the French Quarter.

"No, some weird woman was talking to me. She kept trying to get me to request a reading or something. But I didn't say yes. She told me I was beautiful, which is good to hear from a psychic, I guess."

"How come you didn't want to know?"

"I got my tarot cards read once, and it freaked me out."

"What were the cards?"

"Well, one was the death card."

"No, that's actually a good card."

"How is that a good card?"

"It means you're going to have a new beginning."

"Well then, I guess it was true since a few months after that reading happened, Matt and I broke up."

"See, the card was correct!"

"I'd rather not know and take my chances."

"Yeah, okay, I get that. But what if it's the love card? I'd want to know that so that I can at least be on the lookout."

"Nahh, that's okay. The guys going to have to know that I'm a mess from the get-go. I don't want him to have any surprises. Plus, I'm not really the type that's into that sort of stuff. My friend, Allison, is obsessed with past lives. She actually took Friday off work and was able to drive me to the airport because she was planning to do an ayahuasca session to learn more about her past lives. She's part of some group that does it once a month."

"How cool! Why don't you go?"

"The idea of vomiting for hours does not interest me. Plus, there's too much drama and confusion happening in this current life. I don't need to know about the past ones."

"Ha-ha, okay, fair enough."

"Let's stop here for a minute. I want to grab some snacks for tonight," Joan said as they walked toward a store called Rouses Grocery.

The store was small and crowded. Most of the patrons had king cake or alcohol in their baskets. Lisa and Gabby walked down the chip aisle and grabbed a few bags of Zapp's. Joan was the only one thinking like a responsible adult and came around the corner holding a medium-sized veggie platter and said, "I figured we should have some type of nutrition this weekend. Meet me at the register, I want to grab a bottle of wine, grab a king cake, too, please, Gabs."

As the ladies stood in the checkout line, John entered the store. "Look, it's Dad," Gabby said.

"Hey, hunny," John replied.

"Hey, babe. What are you getting?" Joan asked.

"Beer, gotta get some more for tonight," John said as he made a beeline toward the beer aisle. He knew exactly where he needed to go. The ladies waited for him to complete his purchase before they all walked out together. Right as they exited the store, they were stopped by a wall of people watching a marching band pass by.

"What's going on?" Gabby asked.

"It's a walking parade, usually called a second line." Joan continued, "Small brass bands can be reserved, and you can have yourself your own parade. They are mainly used for events such as parties, weddings, and funerals. During Mardi Gras, they have walking krewes and sometimes use marching bands, like this one. They throw beads and other special throws, but these ones just walk in the quarter."

The krewe that was walking was an all-men's krewe. They were dressed very dapper. They wore sport coats with a crest of their organization on it, some had cigars, and all of them had their booze of choice in hand. They still managed to throw beads and handkerchiefs to revelers standing on the street and up onto balconies. A man in the parade walked up to Gabby and handed her a handkerchief. "For the lovely young lady," he said as he tossed a handkerchief to Gabby, which she happily accepted.

Suddenly, the parade paused, the music slowed, the drums began to rumble, and the woodwinds played low building up to the hook. Revelers lined the street and watched from the balconies to see what was happening and why the parade had paused. Then with the rumble of the drums and explosions of the trumpets, every reveler who recognized the song screamed out "SWEET CAROLINE, BA, BA, BA." Everyone sang loudly and danced in the streets and on the balconies above. The men who were part of the parade twirled women on the sidelines while everyone continued to sing along, "SO GOOD, SO GOOD, SO GOOD, SO GOOD."

Joan, John, Lisa, and Gabby sang loudly and danced; they had jumped onto the street and become part of the parade, with the rest of the revelers. John had opened the box of beer and pulled out a can to start drinking it. He held the box in one hand and a beer in the other. The parade had turned into a massive street party. It was the type of moment that can only happen in New Orleans. Once the parade started to roll onward, there was a gap in the crowd, allowing for Lisa and her family to cut across to reach Canal Street and walk back to their hotel to rest and prepare for Bacchus.

# CHAPTER 12

## *Siesta Time*

"WELL, THERE'S NOT one in here," Joan said, defeated that her search around the hotel room for a corkscrew turned up empty. Gabby and John started to eat the king cake; they did not want to waste any time to dig into the traditional Mardi Gras treat.

"I'll run down and have the bar open it for us," Lisa said.

"Good call, thank you, Lisa," Joan said as she handed Lisa the bottle of wine they purchased from Rouses.

The hotel was quiet. Lisa felt like she was in Spain during siesta time, when everyone goes home to take midday lunch naps. As she got to the lobby and walked to the bar, she was surprised to find that the bar was closed.

"You need help with something, Lisa?" Marcus asked from the concierge desk that faced the bar.

"Hey, Marcus! Yeah, I need a corkscrew."

"I can help you with that," he said as he approached her. He grabbed the bottle from her hand and took it behind the bar to open it. "How many wine glasses do you need?"

"Five," Lisa was accounting for Steve and Vivian.

"All right, here. I don't see a cart," Marcus said as he looked around the bar. "Do you mind carrying two of the glasses?" Marcus asked.

"Not at all," Lisa said as she took two wine glasses from Marcus as he handed them over from the other side of the bar. They walked out of the bar and toward the elevators.

"How was Endymion last night?" Marcus asked.

"It was great! It's crazy how fancy some of the outfits were, considering we were dodging beads and spilling beer all over ourselves. It was a wild and great time."

"Yeah, it's a bit of a contradiction," Marcus responded. "Tonight, the parade is going to come in front of this place, so hopefully I'll be able to catch some beads too."

The elevator arrived to the ninth floor. Lisa was able to get the key out of her back pocket and entered the room where her family members were relaxing on their beds. Joan was watching *The Great British Bake Off*.

"We can put the stuff on the desk."

"Perfect!" Joan said as she got up from the bed. She walked over to her purse to grab some tip money.

"Thank you very much, Marcus," Lisa said.

"Yes, thank you," Joan said while handing Marcus a tip.

"Thank you, ma'am. Is there anything else I can get for you?"

"Nope, I think we're good."

"Enjoy your evening, if you think of anything else you need, then call the concierge," Marcus said before exiting the room.

"That was nice of him to come up with those glasses," Joan said while pouring the wine into two glasses, one for her and Lisa.

"Can I have some?" Gabby asked slyly while not even glancing away from her phone.

"No," John said, his face down into the pillow, trying to take a nap.

Lisa felt her phone vibrate from a text. Her heart skipped a beat. *Mike?* she thought and hoped the text was from him. She looked at her phone, it was Allison. *Okay, second best*, she thought as she sat on her bed.

ALLISON: Hey, girl!

LISA: Hey! You all recovered from ayahuasca?

ALLISON: Getting there. How's Mardi Gras?

LISA: Amazing! You need to come with me next year. You'd love it.

ALLISON: I can't wait to hear all the stories.

LISA: Girrrl, I met a guy!

ALLISON: !!!!!!!!!!!!!!! do tell me more!!!

LISA: Yeah, we met at the masquerade ball and danced all night. When the party ended, I gave him my number, we'll be watching the parade from the same area again tonight, so luckily, I get to see him again!

ALLISON: OMG, that's so sweet! A masquerade ball! That sounds like a fairy tale!

LISA: Yeah, he's super cute and nice. I like him a lot, I can't stop thinking about him.

ALLISON: Have you talked to him today?

LISA: A little bit, he checked in to see what I was up to and confirm I was going back to the same area to watch the parade.

ALLISON: He's thinking of you! That's a good sign.

LISA: Yes, so I'll keep you posted on what all happens. But I'm so glad I came here, this trip has already helped so much!

ALLISON: I'm glad! Okay, I'll let you get to it. Let me know what happens! Sorry I can't pick you up tomorrow. But your car is safe.

LISA: No worries! Thanks for keeping an eye on it.

ALLISON: Love and Light

LISA: Love and Light

Lisa put her phone on the nightstand. She was happy to talk to Allison and grateful for her never-ending friendship and support. Lisa had noticed that the best thing about this hard phase was realizing how great her friends are. She felt happy and continued to drink her wine and watch TV. *Buzz.* Lisa's phone made a noise. She looked quickly, she hoped to see a text from Mike, but it was just an ESPN sports update from the Real Madrid game. She smiled. *Girl, chill, you'll see him soon.* She connected the phone to her charger and set it back on the nightstand. She stared out the window to the sunny sky and wondered what he was doing and who he was with.

# CHAPTER 13

## Bacchus

*KNOCK, KNOCK, KNOCK.* The sounds of the knocking on the door caused Lisa to slowly open her eyes right before Joan answered the door. It was Steve and Vivian. Steve had a small wheeled cooler that he pulled behind him. He held an open beer in one hand that sat snug in an Endymion cozy that he caught the previous night, and a sealed can in the other. As soon as he saw John laying on the bed watching *The Great British Bake Off,* Steve tossed him the unopened can of beer. Vivian was dressed in jeans, sneakers, a black coat, with a green shirt, and a single gold string of starter beads with larger white balls painted to look like pearls.

"Buenas tardes, Perez people!" Vivian said as she entered the room.

"Hey," Lisa said before she yawned, still groggy and waking up from a much-needed nap. *Vivian could wear anything and still look glamourous,* Lisa thought as she saw Vivian and Steve walk through the door. Joan was the only member of the Perez family that had energy. She was singing a Mardi Gras song while she was getting ready.

"It's Mardi Gras time. Time to catch throws. I didn't catch throws, but that's all right because I'm feeling fine, feeling fine, feeling fine," Joan sang repeatedly as she was tying her shoelaces.

Vivian, Joan's life-long hype girl, sang along and bobbed her head a bit to Joan's singing while she touched up her lipstick in the full body mirror in the room. Lisa went into the bathroom to freshen up. She threw some water on her wavy hair and started freshening up her makeup with more care than she would usually do prior to hours of drinking and watching parades. Lisa felt nervous. She was going to see Mike again and wanted to make a solid first impression without the glitz and glamour of a formal ball. Even though they had met the previous night, Lisa couldn't hide behind a mask. She was in her normal clothes, not a fancy ball gown; tonight, it was just Lisa. Lisa took one large yoga breath, *Inhale 1,2,3,4. Exhale 1,2,3,4,* she counted to herself then exited the bathroom back to the common area. Gabby walked in as soon as Lisa exited.

"Is your friend going to be there tonight, Lisa?" Steve asked.

Coyly, she responded, "Oh, the guy from last night? Yeah, they're going to be there again."

"Great, it'd be cool to talk to them more. He seemed like a good enough lad," Steve said before taking a drink of his beer.

"I'm ready!" Gabby announced as she exited the bathroom.

"Bring it on, Bacchus!" John hollered as he got out of the bed and started to put on his shoes.

Lisa and Joan grabbed their bags of snacks then exited the room. The hotel was bustling; it was officially at max occupancy. People were checking in quickly then leaving their suitcases for the bellhop to deliver them to their rooms. Everyone needed to get to their optimal parade positions.

"Have a good evening, Ms. Perez," Marcus said as Lisa and her family walked past the concierge desk.

"Thanks, Marcus, you too," she responded.

Lisa and her family hurried to the St. Charles Hotel. The streets were already barricaded and created a maze for them to walk through in order to get to the other side of the street. As they neared the hotel, Lisa noticed a stark difference between last night and tonight. Instead of dozens of people in formal attire, revelers at the St. Charles Hotel were dressed casually. The ballroom and balcony were still open for revelers, but there was no catered dinner or live jazz band. There were just places for people to sit and catch beads. Lisa and her group sat on the bleachers. The king cakes were stacked one on top of another. Lisa counted a stack of three king cake boxes that Steve brought out to stack on the bleachers next to their crew. Joan got out their box and sat it on top of the stack to share with anyone who wanted a piece. Lisa noticed a box that said "Vietnamese Bakery" written on the side.

"Is this a Vietnamese king cake?" Lisa asked Vivian excitedly.

"Yes, there's a Vietnamese bakery here that makes really good king cakes. So, I thought I'd order one for y'all to try."

"I think I saw something about that on the Food Channel actually. How did you get one?" Joan said as she stood up to cut a slice.

"Viv sent me at 6:00 AM to get that thing. There was already a line of at least thirty people when I got there. But it's true, it's really good and worth the effort," Steve said.

Lisa opened the box and cut a slice. The dough was light and flaky like a croissant, it had cream cheese filling and cream cheese frosting. It was rich, delightful, and incredibly French. "Vietnamese bakeries are my favorite because they are French but not expensive."

"They're French?" Gabby asked while cutting herself a slice of the Vietnamese king cake.

"Yes, all the bakeries are French because Vietnam was colonized by France for so long that the food has a heavy French influence. I live close to an area called little Saigon. Whenever I want to pick up French pastries or a baguette for tapas, I'll just head to little Saigon instead of the fancy and expensive bakeries in the more affluent areas."

"Wow, I never would've guessed, but that makes total sense," John said as he cut himself a slice of the Vietnamese king cake. "Vivian, I have a serious question. Are y'all a neutral-ground family or a sidewalk-side family?" John asked before taking a bite of the cake.

"The only side is sidewalk side," Vivian smugly responded.

"What's that mean?" Lisa asked.

"Neutral ground is that middle area in a street," Vivian said, having a hard time recalling the name.

"A median?" Gabby responded.

Vivian finished her bite of king cake then continued, "Yeah, that's it. Here, we call it neutral ground. People will post up and watch parades from either the sidewalk or the neutral ground. It's a big debate as to what side is best. We pick the sidewalk."

"We don't care. You are the one that is partial toward it," Steve commented.

"Exactly, we are a sidewalk-side family," Vivian said confidently.

"Sounds like a serious topic," Gabby said in a sarcastic tone.

"It is a highly debated subject that is known to cause rifts in friendships and families," Vivian said.

"Has it caused a rift in yours?" Lisa asked.

Vivian continued, "I know my friend Debbie would have an easier time if her in-laws were a neutral-ground family."

"See, that's why I stay out of these sorts of decisions. I know my lane," Steve said.

Lisa sat on the bleachers and took in her environment. It was sunny but cold, she could smell alcohol in the air. She took in the pre-parade of revelers walking along the parade route trying to get to their optimal positions. After a group of drag queens dressed as Dolly Parton walked by, she noticed a row of ladders that were lined up across the street next to a park. The ladders were painted a variety of colors with names written on the boxes that were attached to the tops.

"What are those?" she asked. "Are those ladders?"

"Yeah, people will put their kids on them. They get buckled up and fit into those boxes sort of like in a grocery cart. It gives the kids optimal parade-watching views. I love them with all the parades and festivals here. It's the best thing to save your arms," Vivian explained.

"Is that what you talked about earlier while we were shopping, the color of that ladder, is that also French Quarter green?"

"Yes, exactly," Joan replied.

Lisa sat and continued to take in the surroundings of the city-wide tailgate party. She quickly started to feel anxious to see Mike again. She walked over and put her phone in the side pocket of the cooler so she wouldn't be tempted to text him. She grabbed a beer and sat next to Gabby who was watching a group of kids tie strings of beads together and jump rope in the street. The pre-parade of drunks walking along the parade route was nearly as entertaining to watch as the actual parade. A few other kids threw footballs to each other in the middle of the street that they had caught from the parade, Thoth, that rolled by earlier in the day. Across the street, there was a group of guys playing corn hole, and there was a sign-up sheet for anyone else that wanted to play.

"So, Gabs, any idea what you want to do when you graduate?" Lisa asked Gabby as they sat next to each other on the bleachers.

"I have no idea. My dad says I need to get a job if I don't go to college, or military, or do some type of trade like cosmetology school."

"What interests you?"

"Nothing, so maybe over summer, I'll get a job as a waitress somewhere. I think I'd be good at it. Well maybe not good, I could be okay, just an okay waitress."

"Okay is all you need. I got the ranking of 'meets expectations' on my performance review, and I still got a bonus and raise. So, I will gladly take an okay rating. I don't care either, my boss is a prick who treats us like we're in middle school. I'm surprised he hasn't made my team e-mail him asking permission to use the restroom," she said as she rolled her eyes. "I feel you though. I don't even know what I want to be any more either. Maybe just find a place that won't make you hate waking up every morning, or a place that will make you feel like you have a purpose that helps to feed your potential," Lisa said before taking a sip of her beer.

Lisa looked down St. Charles Avenue, taking in the spectacle of revelers walking around. Then suddenly, she saw him, she recognized his smile. Mike was walking in the middle of the street with his friends. He was holding one handle of a cooler while Moose was holding the other. He was wearing a gray pullover, a Seattle Mariners baseball cap, and a string of green starter beads. Accompanied by Moose and Ric, he looked even more handsome dressed casually than in the tuxedo. She pretended to not notice that he was walking toward her direction and quickly turned her head to stare at the other side of St. Charles Avenue before he could notice that she was staring at him.

She devised a plan to make him see her. "I need to get my phone," she said as she stood up. She grabbed her phone from the cooler. She looked and saw a text from Mike that read, *On our way.* She smiled and wrote back, "We're here." She walked over to the barricade to be in clear view of him as he entered the bleacher area.

"This is a good spot," Mike said as he stood next to Lisa.

"Yeah, prime, real estate right in front. How was your day?" Lisa felt her cheeks get hot, she quickly glanced away to watch a man dressed in a bright green bodysuit walk by so he couldn't see her blush.

"It was cool, I studied for most of the afternoon. We all just decided to take it easy to prepare for tonight."

"Hey, Mikey, here's a beer for ya," John said as he stood next to them. Mike shook hands with John and accepted the beer.

"Thank you," he said as he opened the can and took a drink.

Ric and Moose saw Steve and set up their camp next to the Perez camp. Ric came and shook John's hand and said hi to everyone. Joe and Melissa arrived carrying a large cooler and more snacks. Both groups greeted each other and joined forces.

The stack of king cakes had grown taller to eight cakes. It was a totem pole of pastry that nearly reached the height of Lisa's chin. Lisa's feet were already getting tired. She went to sit on the bleachers. She sat next to Moose, who was sitting and eating a hot dog.

"You look nice today, Moose. I like the black pullover. It looks very chic," Lisa commented.

With a very large grin on his face, he responded, "Thank you, Lisa, I appreciate that."

"You're welcome," Lisa responded in a curious way. She knew something was up, but she was not in on the joke.

"Hey, Joe!" Moose hollered. As Joe turned around, Moose gave him the middle finger.

"See, look at this, this is how you dress," Moose said while motioning to his outfit. "Even Lisa thinks so. She just said this pullover looked nice and chic, yeah chic okay. Not like you, you look like you're about to go bowling."

Joe stared at Moose blankly, wearing something very gaudy a dad would wear. Jeans, tennis shoes, and a button-up short sleeved shirt straight from some movie from the '90s. The shirt was beige with a geometric design and lightly wrinkled. Melissa and Lisa smiled at Moose, trying not to laugh.

"Okay, fine, the next time I go shopping, I will bring you with me to help me make the right choices. You will be the Cher to my Ty in all things fashion and elocution," Joe responded.

"Actually, I think Joe wins the most bonus points now for referencing the movie *Clueless*," Lisa said.

Mike walked over and sat next to her. "Yeah, they had a bit of a fashion debate right before we left, so I'm glad you were here to provide your input on tonight's episode of *Project Runway*," Mike said.

"I have been trying to get rid of that thing for years. I refuse to iron it anymore, which actually works in my best interest since it forced him to learn how to iron," Melissa said as she sat in the empty row in front of them.

"Jokes on you, wife, since I actually enjoy ironing now," Joe responded before taking a drink of beer.

"Really? I hate ironing," Lisa responded.

"Something about seeing the wrinkles disappear is therapeutic for me," Joe said with a bit of a laugh.

"Well, I'm glad I could help settle the debate," Lisa said before she took another sip of her beer. They sat, waiting and observing. A guy walked by and gave Lisa a smile and lingered for a bit hoping to get her attention. He was good-looking but not her type.

"Hey, Lis, look at him, he's looking at you," Steve said, already a bit inebriated.

"Ewe, no."

"No!" John shouted. "He looks nice, like he might have a nice, big truck."

"Definitely not."

"Come on, why not? You're single now, go on and get back out there," John kept prying.

"Because guys with big trucks, that's all they can talk about," Lisa responded.

"Yeah, almost as bad as a man with a plane. Unlike someone I know," Joan said, referring to John.

"Hey, now, planes are way cooler than trucks. My plane is my baby."

"Thanks, Dad," Gabby commented.

"What kind of plane do you have?" Mike asked.

"Grumman AA-5 single propeller," John responded, ready to give every glowing little detail of his plane like a pageant mom.

"Look, he's starting now," Joan said out loud.

John realized that he was about to get into technical pilot terms, so he stopped his train of thought and kept it simple.

"Awesome!" Mike responded.

"So, Mike, are you interested in any particular type of law?" Steve asked.

"I like policy as well as advocating for veterans with disabilities. Maybe I'll eventually go into that for the Air Force or the government."

"Air Force, lawyer, veterans' rights, sounds like the perfect résumé for becoming a senator or a president."

"That would be cool, but my life is a little less than perfect for politics."

"Nonsense, besides the bar is not set too high for politicians these days. All you need is a few million dollars."

"That is true. I guess I should go after things that I'm clearly not qualified for."

"Life is all about taking risks," John said while holding up his beer as if he was giving a toast.

Mike and Steve held up their beers in a small toast before taking a drink. The power trucks passed by, signaling the parade is near. Everyone cheered and stood up and went into their prime parade positions.

"Who'd have thought you could get excited seeing a big bulky Edison Company power truck," Melissa commented.

Lisa leaned over to Joan and Vivian who were in between conversations and asked Joan, "Bacchus, the Greek god of the drink and partying. Is this another super krewe?"

"Yeah, they don't have as many riders as Endymion. But it is equally as fun. Bacchus was the first parade to have a celebrity king, and there are more famous people that ride in it too. The man who started it owns the famous restaurant, Brennan's. When it first started, it broke with a lot of traditions since it let outsiders such as people from out of state ride in it. But it further expanded the joy of the season in my opinion," Joan explained.

The police motorcade combed the streets to make sure the path was clear before the parade arrived. The real knights in shining armor rode before the parade and the king. In traditional Mardi Gras style, the flambeaux came walking by as the first krewe to officially kick off the parade.

A marching band walked by playing "When the Saint's Come Marching In." A group of knights riding horses throwing doubloons was up next. The doubloons sparkled as they flew in the air in the evening lights like fireflies.

"Bacchus started the doubloon tradition. Sometimes they make special doubloons made of real silver that are potentially worth a lot of money. That's why whenever I see a doubloon in the street, I'll take an extra glance to see if it's a special one." Mike leaned in and told Lisa closely since the noise was loud.

Lisa looked toward her left down the street lined as far as the eye could see with revelers. She could see a line of floats lighting up the parade route, with spotlights and confetti that fell slowly from the sky like snow. Will Farrell arrived on his large parade float, the size of a semitruck; it was large, gold, white, with glowing lights that made it sparkle and glisten. There was a large red crown atop it, creating a canopy over the throne for the king to sit on. But the king was standing, waving to the crowd who was dressed in royal regalia. The float reminded Lisa of the painting she saw while in Versailles of the coronation of King Louis XVI. He waved at the crowd and threw beads, he looked overwhelmed and inebriated. Everyone yelled and clapped for him. Bacchus had officially begun. Dozens of throws flew from the floats on the parade route. The floats were decorated in grapes, wine, and other alcohol bottles, as well as any other theme associated with the god Bacchus. Confetti and spotlights were their introduction and their aftermath. There was a massive conglomerate of throws that were aimed toward Gabby and Lisa.

"AHHHH!" Lisa hollered. A string of beads had been thrown so hard they left welts on her hand. After the float passed, there was a large gap in the parade. Lisa put the string of beads around her neck and examined her hand.

"Ouch!" Vivian said. "Here, take a tequila shot, that will take the edge off it."

Lisa obliged; she wanted to do anything to reduce the pain. As she pounded it down, Ric noticed and clapped his hands at Lisa's triumphant shot of tequila. Mike took a step closer to her. She looked up at him, and they locked eyes; for a small moment, the pain had completely dissipated before being interrupted by a loud noise.

BROM, CLICK, TAP, TAP, TAP, CLASH.

BROM, CLICK, TAP, TAP, TAP, CLASH.

BROM, CLICK, TAP, TAP, TAP, CLASH.

The sousaphones, drums, and cymbals of the marching band approaching sounded like an invasion. It was so loud and powerful it caused Lisa, Mike, and the rest of the revelers to look down the street to see the source of the noise.

"Incoming," Mike said as a parade float followed the marching band.

The float was a large pirate ship. The riders were dressed like pirates tossing throws as if the boat was too heavy, and in order to avoid sinking, they were tossing their booty over the sides. Every reveler around Lisa and Mike prepared for the float to come to their section and unload dozens of throws onto their area. The float rolled by rather quickly, leaving beads, go-cups, plastic roses, and doubloons in its wake. Gabby had caught a rose and put it in her hair. Lisa had managed to catch a few beads and put the nicer strings on her neck. The others she put away in the designated bead bag her family had brought with them. The ones she wanted to keep, she'll sort through later, but for now, everything that was caught either went around her neck or inside the bag. Vivian and Joan sat down on the bleachers. The famous New Orleans front porch culture was out on the streets and doing what it does best by creating community and fellowship among neighbors. Everyone was engaging with the world in front of them and around them, no one stuck to their cliques, everyone shared with open arms and open minds.

"Here, Joanie, take another," Vivian said as she handed Joan a shot of tequila.

"Oh, man, I can't any more, Viv," Joan said, and as she took the glass, they touched their glasses together and shouted "Prost!" before they both downed the shot of tequila.

"My goodness, Vivian, has anyone ever told you that you're," she grimaced as she tried to adjust after the shot, "that you're a bad influence?" Joan said.

"Every mother of every guy I ever dated from the age twelve to twenty-four," Vivian responded.

"Ha-ha, yeah I could see that."

"But I don't quite buy into people being a bad influence. You takin' a shot is all on you."

"So, instead of you influencing, you are just my friend who makes bad choices, and people either want to join in the choices or not?"

"Exactly! Just don't mention that to my kids. I don't want them hanging around any of those troublemakers."

"Yes, very true, bad influences and troublemakers are a different scenario. Troublemakers can get you guilty by association."

"Exactly," Vivian responded as she poured another shot of tequila for them both. "PROST!" they both yelled before they took down another shot of tequila.

A float with a band approached, it was a band that Lisa recognized, The Three Brothers; Lisa's favorite blue grass band. "Oh my god! Oh my god! I love this band!" Lisa yelled as she giddily jumped up and down like a little girl and quickly rushed the barrier in hopes to catch a string of beads from their float. They were throwing beads as their music played over the speakers from the float. She sang the lyrics to the song that was playing as they passed by on their float.

The guitarist was on the front of the float throwing beads, he pointed to Lisa and threw a string of beads directly to her. Lisa snatched the beads out of the air like a bridesmaid fighting for a bouquet at a wedding. "Oh my god, he threw them straight to me!" She held the string of plain gold beads in the air to show her family and everyone around before she put them on her neck.

"That string is so basic, how are you going to tell it's from him later on?" Joe commented.

"Oh, I will remember. Plus, this string is blessed, meaning all the beads touching it are now blessed," Lisa said with a smile on her face, aware of how absurd she sounded but partially believing the string was special as well.

Another float rolled by, it was in the shape of a large alligator that was the length of a basketball court. The alligator had red eyes that glowed and was dark green with a bright string of LED lights that outlined its open mouth and along its scaly back. The gator's mouth was open wide and glowed brightly in magenta; a net was covering its mouth to keep revelers from throwing beads into it. The riders were wearing alligator suits and masks that made it look like they were babies riding along its mothers back. The riders had plenty of throws including stuffed alligators.

"Oh, I want one!" John yelled out along with some of the kids that were around. He stood close to the barrier waving his free hand at the riders on the float in hopes to get their attention to throw him one. Finally, one guy noticed him and specifically threw a stuffed alligator to him.

"Babe, why do you want a stuffed alligator?" Joan hollered out to John.

"For Dallas to play with."

"You're the one that's gonna be picking up all the stuffing in the house and yard after that dog rips it to shreds."

Lisa's feet began to hurt, so she took a seat a little higher up on the bleachers to stretch her legs. Melissa noticed and decided to follow suit.

"My feet need a rest too," Melissa said as she sat next to Lisa. She asked, "What do you do for work, Lisa?"

"Business analysis. I work for a tech company. I write up the documents that outline the projects and let the engineers know what they need to code. I also send the project status to the testing teams," Lisa explained.

"Oh, cool, did you study that in school?"

"Not at all, my bachelor's is in literature. I graduated during the recession, and this was the only field and industry that gave me a job."

"Is that what you want to do?"

"I'm not sure yet," she said honestly. "I'd love to start my own company. I'm just not sure what in the world that would be. I guess I don't know what I want to be when I grow up. What about you? What do you do?"

"I'm a fourth grade teacher." Melissa smiled.

"Oh wow, how's it like to teach that age?"

"It's fun! They are old enough to pay attention and know what's expected of them, but still young enough to think you're the coolest person."

"My hat's off to you. I'm always amazed by teachers, especially elementary age. I can barely keep the attention of a group of five kids, let alone twenty plus. But not only do teachers keep their attention, they also have the magic to actually teach them a lesson plan."

"Yeah, it can be challenging at times. But most of the time, it's extremely rewarding."

"How long have you guys been stationed here?"

"About two years. We have two more left of this tour, then we'll see where we are sent next."

"How does that work for teaching?"

"I just do contracts by the year. The school district is close to the base and used to the lives of military kids and parents, so they understand."

"What would you say is the biggest challenge facing kids today?" Lisa asked.

Without hesitation, Melissa responded, "Social media."

"Yikes, yeah, that's got to be insane."

"Luckily, my school makes the kids put phones in designated lockers. But it seems like every day I'm having to lecture about online bullying."

"Now that breaks my heart. I was bullied as well, but at least I could escape it when I was at home. With online bullying and cell phones, it's impossible to escape now."

"Yeah, it's tragic, there was a suicide last year at my school. The strangest part is the parents. They're so oblivious whether it's the bully or the bullied. The parents of the bullies didn't know how terrible their kids were to the victim. When the cops and principal showed the parents the messages the kids who did the bullying sent the victim, they were shocked. Parents always want to believe their kids are good, but some of them are not so, there's like a double tragedy of losing multiple children in a sense."

"Gosh, how do you deal with that as a teacher and lecture them?"

"When the suicide happened, I opened up about my own bully experiences, and it seemed to really sink into my class. But I just try to get to their level and not try to lecture like a parent."

"I commend you for what you do. When I was bullied, I never let them see me react. But one time in the seventh grade, I made a comment that they would be sorry when I was in high school and pretty. Which, of course, made them bully me more. But true to form, the three boys that always made fun of me tried to date me in high school and college. I happily rejected them, and to this day, it felt good to reject them."

"Can I use that story for my class?"

"Absolutely! I have others," Lisa said, giggling. "Luckily, I learned good clap backs. When I was in high school, an evil bitch named Cierra Tesser tried to bully me. I can't remember what it was about, I think I said something ditzy, and she called me stupid. And I responded with, 'at least I'm not in the remedial math class like her', then apparently, she went home and cried all night, but at least she left me alone after that."

"Oh my goodness! That's awesome, I wish I was quick witted like that. I'll think of another way to tell the bullies when I need to lecture them in class though. Because honestly, sometimes that's the case, and if they pick on the wrong person, such as someone quick witted like yourself, they can easily become the bullied. But in your case, that bully deserved it, and I'm glad you were able to fight back with your brain."

"It's a blessing and a curse," Lisa responded. "So, girl to girl, is Mike dating anyone? He told me he was single. But you know guys, just how single is he?" she asked.

"Very single," Melissa confirmed. "They play pool in the garage, smoke cigars, and drink beer a few nights a week. They think the walls are thicker than they really are. So, when I want, I can hear some good conversations. He's not even on any dating apps, that's how single he is."

"Okay, good to know. I think I'll go and see what he's up to," Lisa said as she stood up and headed toward where Mike was standing.

"Hey, I caught you this," Mike said as he held up a plastic Mardi Gras Bacchus cup. "Now these are my favorite throws, I have about ten of them at my house. They're the best cups, they are perfect for picnics or outdoor events."

"Why, thank you," Lisa said as she accepted his gift.

"Did you have a nice chat with Melissa?" Mike asked.

"Yeah, she's a cool girl. How'd Joe land a great one like her?"

"I've asked myself that question dozens of times. Naw, Joe's a loyal, great guy and treats her super well. So, I can definitely see what she sees in him."

Lisa stood closer to him now that she had confirmation from a close friend of his singleness; she felt confident to flirt with him and ignite a spark. A float rolled by with a band playing live music, the classic song "Walking to New Orleans." Lisa was the only person who did not recognize the song, everyone around her was singing along, including Mike and his friends.

After the float passed by, the parade came to halt. "Is it over?" Lisa asked Mike.

"No, it's too soon, maybe a float broke down," he responded as he took out his phone.

Lisa stared at his phone to try and get a glimpse of his screen saver photo, but he unlocked it too quickly for her to see if there were any photos.

He said, "According to the app, one of the float engines stalled, the float that was parked in front of where they were sitting had thrown as many throws as they could."

The riders and spectators were hanging out, drinking and eating king cake. They all sat down and waited for the parade to start rolling again. Lisa saw Gabby sitting on the bleachers while rummaging through the bead bags and decided to join her.

"What's that?" Lisa asked Gabby who was examining a black rectangular object that she had caught.

Gabby shook the box; it made a rattling noise like it had something inside of it. "I have no idea," Gabby responded as she tried to open the box that was sealed very well with tape. Finally, she was able to get her fingernail through the box and ripped it open. She was pushing the box hard which caused her hands to move quickly.

Ric, who was sitting next to Gabby, looking at his phone unaware of the situation, said, "Yes, this is the easiest money I'm ever going to make."

"Why is that? Are you finally betting against your team?" Lisa quickly responded.

"That's a good one. I'm gonna remember that one," Mike said as he moved closer to Lisa and Gabby to see what was in the black box.

She blushed; she didn't realize Mike was paying attention to her. She looked at him, and they locked eyes, exchanging smiles like lovers do. Ric, who was still looking at his phone oblivious to what Gabby was doing, saw her hand move quickly in his peripheral. He flinched in surprise and said, "What the hell?"

"What's wrong with you, dude? It's just a box," Melissa said as she observed the situation from where she sat on the bleachers.

"I don't know, man! You can't make quick moves like that around me okay. I'm from Detroit," Ric responded with a nervous laugh. Gabby, Lisa, and Melissa all chuckled in response.

"It's a Bacchus-themed harmonica!" Gabby said as she began to blow into it, trying to play a song.

"You never know what you'll catch here. I'm losing my buzz. Shotgun race?" Ric said as he motioned to their crew.

"Great idea," Joe said as he opened the cooler to get cans of beer out. Joe went around to everyone in their immediate area and gave them all a can but skipping Gabby.

Ric announced, "Everyone who wants to play, circle up. All right, on the count of three, we shotgun these, and whoever finishes first is the winner."

Lisa looked at Mike and whispered, "Are we all doing this?"

"Yes." He wrapped his arm around her and pulled her into the circle. She loved the feeling of being briefly in his embrace.

"Remember how to do this, Mike? You need to use your arm strength. Use muscles like mine to press open the can. It will be hard with your spaghetti arms, but I believe in you," Moose teased.

"Yeah, yeah," Mike responded as he took the can and prepped to open.

"Count us off, Gabby," Ric said.

As the Perez crew, Mike's friends, and a few new people gathered around, Gabby stood next to John and held up the handkerchief she had caught earlier in the walking parade. "Three, two, one, FIGHT CLUB!" Gabby yelled as she waved her scarf to signal the race had begun.

Beer splashed everywhere. Clearly, most of them had not shotgunned beers in years. Lisa felt the cold beer all over her face as she opened the can and the beer flowed unsuccessfully into her mouth.

"Victory!" Joan yelled as she finished first.

John stopped as soon as Joan claimed first place and yelled proudly, "That's my wife!"

"Good lord," Lisa said after she finished shotgunning her beer and wiped her face with her sleeve. "I hadn't shotgunned a beer since college."

"Ha-ha, yeah, it's immature but fun," Mike said.

They all sat down on the bleachers, drank more alcohol, and enjoyed conversation and each other's company until the parade started moving again. The float that was broken down finally caught up with the rest of the parade. A marching band from a local high school followed the float next. They looked tired and spent. They were in between songs and taking a small break from playing and were strictly marching. Until one lone trumpet started playing a familiar song. A few flutes started to play as well. Steve started to sing along in a low voice. Lisa focused for the first time in her life. The lyric "You have found her now go and get her," it resonated in her so intently she felt a chill go down her spine. To her, it was about Mike, which scared her but also excited her. She looked up to where he was sitting, and he was staring at her, smiling, just as he did the previous night at the ball.

*Does he feel the same way?* she thought, as her heart began beating harder. With the scream of the trumpet and tossing of the flags by the color guard, the revelers immediately started singing along, "Nah, nah, nah, nah, nah, nah, nah, nah, nah, hey, Jude."

Every ethnicity, creed, and orientation were in attendance, and every one of them was singing, to the Beatles' song "Hey Jude." The marching band was playing in full gear, the parade was back in motion. Everyone offered each other cheers and smiles while they sang in unison. Even as the marching band passed and a smaller float in the shape of fleur-de-lis came rolling by throwing beads, revelers still sang along to the song as the band continued to play as they walked down the street. "Nah, nah, nah, nah, nah, nah, nah, nah, nah, hey, Jude."

Awake and energized, Lisa handled the last forty-five minutes of the parade like a champion. She caught throws, dodged, throws, ate king cake, Zapp's chips, and drank gallons of libations. She could not remember the last time she experienced an event like Bacchus. She felt exhilarated, alive, and stimulated by the music of the marching bands, colors, and lights of the parade floats. She felt lucky to share this moment with Mike and her family.

After the last parade float rolled past and the fire engine arrived to signal the end of the parade, everyone started to gather their belongings. Mike's friends shook hands and said their goodbyes to Lisa's family and the new friends around them.

Moose came up to Mike and said, "We're going to drop the stuff off at the room then head to the Frenchman. Are you coming?"

"One sec," Mike said.

Lisa glanced over at her family. They looked tired. She could hear them discussing restaurant options.

"Would you like to come out with us tonight?" Mike asked Lisa.

She looked into his eyes and felt a connection, which made her feel conflicted. She desperately wanted to say yes and continue the night with him. However, she decided that it might not be the best decision. She responded, "You know, I really do want to spend this last night with my family, I never see them." She didn't want to say goodbye just yet, she went out on a limb, and in an act of courage, she gave Mike a proposition. "But I have an idea. They leave at 9:00 AM tomorrow, I don't leave until 5:00 PM. I was going to explore the city, check out the music, do some shopping, take pictures, and I'd love to track down a piece of street art. Would you like to join me?"

Mike smiled, his Oscar-winning smile that made Lisa's heart skip, and said, "Yes, that sounds like a fun idea. Where and what time should we meet up at?"

"How about 9:30 AM by touchdown Jesus?"

"Look at you sounding like a local using touchdown Jesus. I like it! 9:30 AM it is."

"Great! Let me say bye to your friends."

"Yeah, let me do the same with your family," Mike said. He stood aside as Lisa said goodbye to his friends.

Lisa walked over to Melissa gave her a hug first and said, "It was nice meeting you! Good luck with these boys."

"Thanks! Great meeting you as well. Have fun during the rest of your trip."

"You're not coming?" Joe asked Lisa.

"Naw, I want to spend this last night with my family. But have fun!"

"All right then," Joe said as he gave Lisa a hug.

"Later, Lisa," Moose said as he gave Lisa a hug.

"Bye, guys, Happy Mardi Gras!" Lisa said after she gave Ric a hug then turned to walk toward her family.

"All right, let me say bye to everyone," Mike walked with Lisa over to her family to say his goodbyes. He shook hands with her uncle and the rest of their crew. "It was great meeting y'all, have a safe trip back home."

"Mike!" Ric hollered.

"I gotta run, see you tomorrow," Mike said to Lisa. He quickly but firmly gave Lisa a hug.

"See you tomorrow!" she said as she held onto him, not wanting to let go of his embrace.

"Okay, have a good night," Mike said while trying not to walk too fast.

"You too," Lisa responded while watching him walk quickly toward his friends.

She felt sad to see him walk away. She wanted to immediately jump into his arms, and into his life; she wanted to dive head first into a relationship with him. But she was ultimately proud that she didn't go with him and risk making a drunken mistake; she was buzzed, and he was drunk. It was best to just wait until tomorrow. They had tomorrow to spend the day together and to learn about each other. She still had tomorrow that will be the granted wish or the grand disappointment.

"Ready, girlie? There's a restaurant not too far from here we're going to grab a quick bite to eat if you want to join us?" Joan said, wanting to give Lisa the option to go with her new friends.

"Yeah, I'll come with you," Lisa said as she grabbed one of the coolers.

"Y'all ready?" John asked Joan and Lisa as he angled his body in the direction of the restaurant.

"Yep," Lisa responded as she started walking toward John.

They walked for two blocks in the French Quarter before they arrived at a restaurant called Bayou Grille. It wasn't anything fancy, just a simple place to grab a bite to eat. The restaurant had long oak tables, long enough to fit everyone perfectly and big enough to keep the coolers and bags of beads under and not crowd the restaurant.

"Welcome, how many are in y'all's party?" the hostess asked Joan.

"Six please," Joan responded.

"Right this way, ma'am," the hostess said as she grabbed a stack of menus, knowing by touch the count of six menus. They sat down at a large square table and started reading the menus. "Your waitress will be here shortly," the hostess said before she walked back to her station.

"What are charbroiled oysters?" Lisa asked.

"They are delicious is what they are Californian," John said while reading his menu.

"Oysters with olive oil, garlic, parmesan cheese. They put them on the grill for a few minutes so they're cooked. Do you like oysters?" Joan asked Lisa.

"They're okay, but that sounds good. I'll give it a try."

"Hello, y'all, my name is Cece, and I'll be your server this evening. What can I get, y'all, to drink?" Cece asked.

Steve and Vivian ordered waters, they needed to start sobering up to drive back to their house. John and Joan ordered beers. Gabby ordered a Coke. Lisa ordered water, she wanted to avoid a hangover for her day with Mike.

"I think everyone's decided on their food orders as well," Vivian said.

"Oh, perfect!" Cece said as she went around the table to also take food orders.

Their party ordered an assortment of creole dishes. Joan and Gabby both ordered the chicken jambalaya. John and Steve ordered boil bags with a side of oysters. Vivian ordered a plate of red beans and rice. Lisa ordered the charbroiled oysters. As they waited for their food, they discussed the night's events, their favorite floats, and the costumes they saw.

Cece approached the table balancing a tray of drinks, she balanced them so well it looked like it was an extension of her arm. As she distributed the drinks, she asked, "Are y'all visiting or do you live here?"

"Well, we used to live here for years, but we're in the military, and now my husband, daughter, and I live in Elizabeth City. They live here on the West Bank," Joan said, motioning to Vivian and Steve. "Vivian grew up here too, she's Cajun."

"That's right, 100 percent, baby," Vivian responded.

"Lisa lives in California," Joan said while motioning to Lisa.

"Ahh, California, beautiful. Is this your first time visiting the Crescent City?" Cece asked.

"Yes, it is, and what a time to visit," Lisa responded.

"Welcome to our Crescent City. It's a good time to visit. Mardi Gras is the time when you get the full experience of our culture."

"I'll be hanging around this area tomorrow. Do you have any recommendations on places to shop at? I want to buy some legit street art."

"Well, honey, tomorrow is your day. Every artist will be out on the streets selling their finest work, especially at Jackson Square. It's the perfect day to do any sort of treasure hunting. Mardi Gras is known as the biggest free party on earth. Let me go and check on y'all's food. In the words of our people, 'Lache pas la patate,'" Cece said as she smiled and held up her hands in the air and walked away.

"What'd she say?" Gabby turned to ask Vivian.

"It's a traditional Cajun phrase. It translates to don't let go of the potato or don't give up."

"Cool, I'm not even going to begin to learn how to say that," Gabby responded.

"I love that phrase, the biggest free party on earth. It's true, this entire weekend has been one giant party," Lisa commented.

A few minutes later, Cece and a busboy came with the trays of food to the table and distributed them appropriately. "Is anything else I can get y'all?"

"Umm, no, I think we're good," Vivian responded.

"All right, bon appétit," Cece said before she walked away.

Steve and John dug into their bags as everyone else at the table began eating their dishes. Lisa stared at her plate of charbroiled oysters. They were golden and smelled delicious and were accompanied by a toasted French baguette. She was a bit confused and was not sure where to start.

"Okay, how do I eat these?" Lisa looked up at Joan, defeated and confused.

"Just dig in with a fork. Stick it in, and they come right out. You can put it on the bread or eat it without the bread," Vivian responded.

Lisa took her fork and stuck it in the middle, she pulled out the oyster and ate it. She loved it. It was the perfect texture. The olive oil was smooth and soft while the parmesan gave it the perfect salty bite. The bit of creole spice gave it the appropriate kick, making the bread the perfect pairing to even it out.

"How are the red beans, Viv?" Joan asked.

"They're okay, I make better. But they're good enough."

"Vivian makes the best red beans and rice. She even won an award for it at the Crescent City red beans and rice festival," Joan explained to Lisa.

"I remember that day. That was the day that we picked up that lost fisherman, and Andy Murphy got beat up by some sixty-five-year-old Vietnamese woman," John said.

"What?" Lisa asked, partially laughing.

"Yeah, we were headed down to the festival, all excited for all the free samples we were going to get, then we got a call to do a rescue. Some fishing boat sent out a distress signal, so we flew out to the gulf, and this man was having a heart attack. His wife was on the boat as well, and she didn't want us to take him, I have no idea why." John continued, "Right as we were rescuing him, she punched Andy, Mike Tyson style, square in the jaw. He was knocked out cold for about five seconds but then came to and took the man and the woman with him to the helicopter. The translator said that she was afraid we were there to arrest him. She apologized profusely to Andy. But, yep, he got KO by an old lady."

"Knowing Andy, he certainly had it coming," Joan said before taking a bite of her jambalaya.

"Yeah, probably, but I never let him forget about it. Whenever he acts out of line, I threaten to send an old lady after him," John said.

"Why do they call it the Crescent City?" Lisa asked.

"The name comes from how the river is shaped. The way the river sort of curves around the city, it makes it look like a crescent. But, of course, it has a lot of nicknames. My favorite is the City of Yes!" Vivian exclaimed.

"I like that one as well. I feel like it's a bit more reflective. I certainly have said yes to a lot of things I normally wouldn't do during the short time I've been here," Lisa added.

"So, how do you like the oysters, Lis?" Joan asked.

"This is pretty much my new favorite food. I could easily eat these oysters every day."

"Well, move here and you can," Vivian added.

"Vivian, you're from here, then you moved around, then came back. What do you like the most about this city?" Lisa asked.

"Oh, man, this is the hometown of my soul. Don't get me wrong, there's plenty I don't like about it, like the poverty and corruption. But there's always a festival, there's always something to do, and we really do have this connection to each other here like nowhere I've seen. There is not a transient vibe that cities like New York, Boston, and Los Angeles have. Where people who are born there don't necessarily stay there, or people come and go during certain seasons or pursuits in their lives."

Vivian added, "It's easy to find people whose families date back generations, and they have no intention of leaving. Like us for instance, some people turn their nose down on New Orleans because of the crime, yet we chose to come back here to raise our kids with the culture and traditions that are only found here. It's like we're in on a secret together. Take Mardi Gras for instance, everywhere else it's only Tuesday. When I'm traveling or when I was stationed in other states or countries, if I meet someone from Louisiana, we're connected through Mardi Gras, we're like instant family."

"Yeah, New Orleans is a wonderful flavor on its own," John said as he was ripping the head off a crawfish.

"Yeah, I totally get what you mean about the transient cities. That's certainly what LA and San Francisco is like with people moving to find their fame and fortunes. Whether it was the gold rush of the 1800s or now with people moving to the cities to make it in tech and entertainment. California will spit you out as quickly as it welcomed you. New Orleans is like the friendly grandmother that invites you in and feeds you immediately, covers you with blankets, and never wants you to leave. I like this city a lot," Lisa responded before she ate another oyster.

Lisa and her crew ate and enjoyed their last meal together before heading back to The Roosevelt. As they walked out of the restaurant, the city was still radiant with life. There were people everywhere. Every bar was packed with people wearing their throws from Bacchus, still drinking and enjoying the night. They walked through the streets, past touchdown Jesus to Canal Street where they crossed into the Central Business District to The Roosevelt. As they entered through the glowing gilded doors, the hotel lobby was still busy with people all around drinking at the Sazerac bar.

"Baby, do you have the valet ticket? I'll get the car brought up now so we don't have to wait too long," Steve asked Vivian. She opened a small zipped pocket on the side of her coat that safely housed the valet ticket.

"Put it on our room again, Steve, it's room 921," John said as Steve got the ticket from Vivian.

"Okay, thanks, man," Steve said, smiling to John before walking to the valet window.

Vivian was taking inventory of their bags, beads, and belongings. When Steve walked back, they all hugged and said their goodbyes. "It was lovely to spend time with you, Lisa. Come back and spend Mardi Gras with us again, ya hear," Vivian said before giving Lisa a hug.

Steve and Vivian walked over to the valet stand to get their car to drive home. Lisa and her family headed upstairs to go to sleep. The weekend was quickly coming to an end. John, Joan, and Gabby had a flight to catch the next morning. But Lisa still had one more day in the City of Yes. She had one more day to learn, indulge, and experience New Orleans. She had one more day to spend with Mike.

# CHAPTER 14

## *Lundi Gras*

HER EYES FELT heavy, and there was a faint pain in her head. Lisa awoke to the sounds of Joan's alarm clock beeping and buzzing, waking her and her hangover. The time was 6:00 AM, it was a miracle that everyone was up and functioning. Lisa's body was sore, she used every muscle she could to get out of bed to walk to her purse that was buried below beads and grab the ibuprofen. She chugged nearly an entire bottle of water before she crawled back into bed to let the medicine kick in. John and Joan began packing their bags, and everyone rotated through the showers. Lisa struggled to get up and get going. She slowly dug out her clothes for the day and began packing her suitcase. Joan exited the bathroom ready to fly home.

"It's all yours," she said to Lisa.

Lisa stood in the warm shower with her face toward the showerhead, allowing the water to wake her up. Lisa was not a high maintenance woman, but she always looked refined and put together. She put more effort into her makeup since she would be spending the day with Mike. After she was done applying her makeup, she joined Gabby in the main room to sort through the drawers of beads and other Mardi Gras throws. They divided up their favorite ones that were worth the space in the suitcases. She'd been a traveler since she was an infant. She rarely packed more than a carry-on. However, this time, she made an exception, she would be checking her carry-on bag when she got to the airport, and her carry-on items would be one giant bag of beads and her purse. She shoved all that she could into her carry-on luggage, including the gifts she had purchased for her friends and family. She made sure she still had enough room in her bags for any purchases to be made while she explored the city with Mike. She took her camera out of her bag, the first time she had done since she arrived. She wanted to take pictures of the city during her last day of exploring. Once the bags were packed and the hotel room was tidied up, the Perez family headed downstairs to the breakfast buffet.

"Do you have any specific plans for today Lisa?" Joan asked.

"Actually, Mike and I are going to hang out and explore the city."

"Lundi Gras is probably my favorite day of Mardi Gras. Man, I wish we didn't have to go back so soon," Joan said.

"Eh, I'm a little paraded out. I'm ready to go back home and relax," John said calmly. "It's a good thing it only happens once a year, by the time you're ready to go to another parade, it's carnival season all over again. I'm glad you were here, kiddo. It's been fun having you with us."

"Thank you for allowing me to come here and stay with you at such short notice. It's been so amazing. I'm glad I came and marked this off of both my lifelong bucket list and my thirty before thirty list. I for sure want to turn this into a tradition."

"You have a thirty before thirty list?" Gabby asked.

"Yep, I started it after the breakup. My therapist friend recommended it since I sort of have a new lease on life now that I'm not getting married anytime soon."

"What else is on it?" Gabby asked.

"Go on a safari in Africa, fly a plane, ski in Switzerland, drink scotch in Scotland, to name a few," Lisa said while using her fingers as counters.

"Well, come visit us, and I'll take you up on my plane so you can cross that one off your list," John responded.

"I certainly will plan on that one, Uncle Johnny," Lisa said.

*Ding,* rang the elevator as they arrived to the lobby. They walked through the opulent five-star gilded lobby toward the Fountain Lounge where breakfast was being served. The lounge was nearly empty with only one other couple enjoying an early morning breakfast.

"Good morning, y'all, welcome to the Fountain Lounge. I'm Sandra, will you be ordering anything special or enjoying our award-winning buffet? Also, if you'd like to charge it to your room, what room are you staying in?"

"Buffet please, room 921, last name Perez," Joan responded.

"Okay, great, go ahead and seat yourselves to where you would like. Can I take your beverage orders?"

"Coffee all around. Chicory coffee for me," Joan said.

"Great, I will bring that right out," Sandra said with a smile, not even having to write anything down.

The Perez family walked over to a large table for four. John put the room key down to lay claim to the table. The buffet had a wide variety to choose from, with every breakfast pastry that could exist, including specialty ones that the chefs at The Roosevelt made specifically themed for Mardi Gras. Chaffing dishes were filled with pancakes, scrambled eggs, French toast, fruit, yogurt, sausage, bacon, as well as crab and shrimp. It was a breakfast fit for a Mardi Gras king. The Perez family sat in peace and started to eat their breakfast. A server had arrived at their table carrying a tray of four coffee mugs and four glasses filled with water, and distributed them appropriately.

"Thank you," everyone said as they received the drinks.

"My pleasure. Is there anything else I can get you?" the server asked professionally and attentively.

"Nope, I think we're good," John replied.

"Great, enjoy your breakfast," the server said with a smile before he walked away from the table. He walked directly to another table that had just sat down.

The family continued to enjoy their breakfast. Lisa had biscuits and gravy, fruit, bacon, hash browns, and drank coffee. John ate crawfish etouffee, bacon, sausage, biscuits, crab legs, shrimp cocktail, hash browns. Joan had crawfish etouffee, fruit, sausage. Gabby ate French toast and fruit.

"What are your final thoughts on Mardi Gras, Lisa?" John asked as he put butter on his biscuit.

"I love it! This has been such an amazing time. Now every parade I go to will not compare. I went to the Rose Parade once, and I thought that was amazing. But that is nothing as exciting as the Mardi Gras parades, and boring in comparison," Lisa said.

"Yeah, you can't drink," Gabby chimed in.

"But there must be lots of celebrities and famous people at the Rose Parade," Joan inquired.

"Yeah, but still no drinking and no throws. Now every time I go to a parade that's not Mardi Gras, I'll have withdrawals and want to be holding a beer, and bored that I can't partake and catch anything."

"Which is how all parades should operate," Gabby responded.

As they continued to discuss the past few days and eat their breakfast, Lisa began to feel sad at the thought of not being able to see them for a while. She felt extremely grateful that she could stay with her family at this magnificent hotel, and the conversations she had with her aunt and uncle, that helped give her the healing she craved.

"All right, ladies, it's time to start heading out," John said as he put the white cloth napkin on the table. He was throwing in the towel to adjourn the weekend. The server walked over to the table to check in on them.

"Is there anything I can get you? May I top off your beverages?" the server asked.

"We'll take the check please," John responded.

"Certainly," the server said as he walked to the hostess desk.

The check was already printed out. The server gave the check to John who quickly examined the bill and signed. He got out his wallet and threw a few bucks on the table as a tip. They all stood up slowly, their bodies were sore and tired. Lisa felt like she had finished an intense sporting competition. They headed back to the room to grab their bags and do one last walk-through to make sure they did not forget anything. Lisa grabbed her belongings. She was packed and didn't have any intention to return to the room once she was out exploring the city with Mike.

"What about the rest of the beads in the drawer?" Lisa asked while pointing to the dozens of beads that filled the dresser drawer to the brim.

"The housekeeping staff will know what to do with them. They'll either keep them for their own collections or send them off to recycling," Joan said.

"That makes me feel so much better that they get taken to recycling," Lisa said.

"Oh yes, they get cleaned up and repackaged. Or used in other parades. One year, I rode in the St. Patrick's Day parade. During Mardi Gras, I only kept the green and gold beads and used those as my throws for my ride. Because if you ride, you have to pay and provide your own beads," Joan explained.

"What does the St. Patrick's Day parade look like?" Lisa asked.

"Like Mardi Gras but gold and green. They throw corned beef, cabbage, and potatoes. One of the riders on my float had boxes of lucky charms she would throw into the crowds," Joan said.

"I need to experience that parade one day. I'm adding that to my list," Lisa added.

They did one last look around the room before heading downstairs to check out.

"Got your chargers, babe?" Joan asked John as they waited for the elevator.

"Gah, let me go back to the room," John said while leaving his luggage.

"I think he's probably lost about twenty chargers from leaving them in hotels all over the world."

"I was reading an article in a travel blog, that if you need a charger, just ask the front desk of a hotel if they have any, because of people like Dad who always leave them behind," Gabby said.

"Oh, good to know! I'll remember that one for one of my trips," Lisa said.

The elevator arrived just in time as John came jogging around the corner, holding a phone charger. They crammed into the elevator between the four of them, luggage, and bead bags; there was little room for anyone else. Not having to leave right away, Lisa walked toward the concierge desk to have her luggage stowed.

"Hi, Marcus!"

"Hey! Good morning, Lisa. What can I help you with?"

"Can I keep my bags stowed here? My plane doesn't leave until later this afternoon."

"Of course," Marcus said as he pulled out a name tag and a pen. He wrote her name and room number on the tag and then took a count of the items she wished to keep stowed. "Hey, really quick, I have something for you," Marcus said before he headed toward the back room. He directed the second concierge to take the bags and put the tags on.

"I want you to have this," Marcus said as he gave Lisa a clear plastic bag with what appeared to be a black ball covered in glitter. "It's a Zulu coconut, a prized possession for the Mardi Gras festival."

"Oh, wow, that is awesome, thank you!" she said as she opened the bag to peek inside. She didn't want to take the whole thing out and get glitter everywhere.

"Wow, that's real neat. Take care of that thing, those are highly coveted," John said.

"I think that's our shuttle," Gabby said.

"Yep, well it's been fun hanging out with you here, girly. Have fun and take lots of pictures," Joan said while giving Lisa a hug.

"Have fun exploring the city. We'll let you know when we land in a couple of hours," John said while giving Lisa a hug.

After hugging John, Lisa moved in to hug Gabby. "Thanks for letting me stay with you, guys, and letting me tag along. This has truly been an incredible weekend."

Her family walked toward the exit doors to where their shuttle was patiently waiting to take hotel guests to the airport. The doorman took their luggage and put it in the back of the shuttle. Before Marcus put her last bag into the locked closet, she opened a small opening in her bead bag and carefully placed the Zulu coconut inside.

"What time should I have an airport shuttle here for you?" Marcus asked.

"Well, my flight is at 7:30 PM. What time should I leave here by?"

"Four thirty, with the parades, traffic, and street closures, that would be a safe time to leave and not worry about being late or missing your flight."

"Okay, 4:30 PM then."

"Perfect, it will be here ready for you. You go on and enjoy yourself, Ms. Perez."

"Thanks, Marcus!" Lisa said.

She started to walk through the bustling lobby of the historic Roosevelt Hotel, taking pictures of the statues, floral arrangements, and gold decor. As she walked outside, she took in a deep breath of air that officially eradicated her hangover. The air was crisp, the clouds hung low in the sky. They were spread out wide enough for there to be more sunlight than dark patches. The bottoms of the clouds were dark gray. The tops of the clouds sparkled like platinum with high white peaks that looked like a merengue pie. The sunshine was bright but not overpowering. It was the gentle winter sun that provided just enough light to brighten one's mood and provide the freedom to walk around with ease and comfort, but not bright enough to wear sunglasses. As Lisa walked around the city, she took pictures of the magnolia trees, streetcar lines, and streetlamps that were covered with beads. As she crossed Canal Street toward the French Quarter, she noticed that a lot more people were in the city than she saw yesterday. Most of the tourists and first timers had arrived for Fat Tuesday.

She continued to walk along Royal Street until she was greeted by iron fencing and the greenery of the church cemetery. She scanned her surroundings, looking in both directions of the street, but she didn't see Mike anywhere. She started taking pictures of the cemetery. She zoomed her lens in and out, trying to get a closer view of touchdown Jesus. The fencing kept people from getting close to the statue. She was taking pictures of the fleur-de-lis tops of the posts and the old tombstones that were in the cemetery. She had fun playing around with the different settings and seeing which one worked well with the lighting. She used the zoom in her lens to read the tombstones. She noticed one tombstone that had black Xs all over it. She didn't know what it was or why it was like that.

"Good morning!"

She jumped, the voice surprised her and caught her off guard; it was Mike. She looked up from her lens and saw him walking toward her from Canal Street.

"Buenos días!" Lisa responded.

"That's a nice camera," he commented.

He was dressed casually, sporting his Mariners hat again. She was dressed casually under her winter coat. Sporting the new tank top Joan bought her and Gabby. She accessorized with starter beads and her new fleur-de-lis necklace. Her hair was down and wavy. Her California cool was showing in the Cajun country.

"Is photography your art?"

"Hmm, maybe, I just love nice pictures. Whenever I travel, I print my favorite scenery pictures and frame them. I have a vision for my house to have a hallway of framed pictures of everywhere I've been."

"Good camera," he said while inspecting it.

"It was my college graduation gift from my parents."

When Mike handed the camera back to her, she noticed a very large scar on his hand and forearm. She wanted to inquire about it, but it didn't seem like the appropriate time.

"*Laissez les bons temps rouler*. Let the good times roll," Mike said as he read her shirt. "Nice shirt!" he commented. "That is probably my favorite New Orleans saying."

"Thanks, once my aunt translated the meaning, I had to get it. Hey, question, while I was looking around, I saw a tombstone with a bunch of Xs. What is it? Why are there Xs all over it?"

"That's Voodoo Queen Marie Laveau's tombstone. Legend has it, that if you visit her grave and make a wish, you must draw an X on her stone. Look again through your lens," Mike said, motioning for Lisa to look in her camera. Lisa obliged and looked through her lens toward the tombstone. "Let me know when it's in focus again," Mike said.

"Okay, I got it now," Lisa said while peering through her camera lens. She took a picture then took the camera away from her face to examine it on the screen. Mike stood closer to her to get a glimpse of the picture.

"Do you see some of the Xs have circles around them?" he said as he pointed to the Xs in the photo with circles around them.

"Yeah, a few," she said as she zoomed in.

"If your wish comes true, believers will come back and circle the X they made."

"Interesting. How do people get in there?" Lisa asked.

"Through tours, some people break in, but if you get caught, it's a pretty hefty fine. Apparently, some members of the band Misfits broke in here and tried to steal her body. But people around said that they just jumped the fence and had a small party before the cops came. There's a lot of old New Orleans stories and folklore tied to her."

"Yeah, I went into her shop," Lisa said.

"Did you get a voodoo doll?"

"No, it's not my thing. Gabby did though, so watch out for her."

"I was wondering why she asked for a lock of my hair. Did you already eat?"

"Yeah. Did you?"

"A little, but I could go for a Bloody Mary brunch. Wanna go get one?"

"Sure, lead the way," she shrugged.

They turned the corner in the direction of Jackson Square. Lisa was pleasantly surprised to see the square thriving with musicians and street artists. The artists had their booths set up, and their art was positioned along the fencing of the perimeter of Jackson Square park. The artists sold various paintings of the cathedral and other New Orleans inspired pieces to both locals and tourists.

"Jackpot! Hold up one second, let me check the booths for my painting," Lisa said while veering off their designated path toward the displays.

"Painting?" Mike asked. "There are some galleries over there," Mike said as he pointed to some shops.

"No, it has to be from the street. It's one of my things. Wherever I travel, I need to buy legit street art," Lisa said while looking through the paintings of one of the booths lining the fencing of Jackson Square park.

"Interesting, why?" Mike asked as he held up a large canvas of a saxophone player watercolor.

"Because street artists get a view of everyone and everything. They observe the locals walking around carrying on everyday life. They also observe the tourists getting a fresh take on this city. I always feel a sense of truth when I see their work. Plus, I can get to talk to them as well and learn their stories. When I was living in Spain, there was a man selling pictures on the street made of butterfly wings. He was an immigrant from Senegal just trying to work and save enough money to bring the rest of his family to Spain. He worked in a store and on the weekends sold his work on the paseo. He was a good man, with a good heart and an amazing talent. His work sits on my desk in my room. Where else can you speak and connect with an artist like that other than on the street?" Lisa looked at a booth of watercolors of saxophone players; she felt like she found her piece. She felt like she had found one of her many treasures during the day's hunt. As she examined the rest of the table, she saw a sign the artist posted that read "The Role of the artist is to see the world and describe it."

"Case in point, look at that sign," Lisa said as she nudged Mike and pointed to the sign. "This artist's paintings are a representation on how he sees the world that surrounds him. Look at all the uses of color that surround these saxophone players. It captures and depicts the movement of the player. The multiple colors surrounding him are improvised just like a jazz song."

"Wow, I think I have a new appreciation for street art now!" Mike said.

Lisa stared at the picture for a little longer, but she wasn't quite ready to buy it. She continued to walk around and look at the other booths. She admired the different styles and techniques of each painting. No two paintings were alike.

"So, you're a traveler? Quick, how many passport stamps do you have? A real traveler always knows that number," Mike asked Lisa in a quick manner, like a game show host.

"Twenty-six," she responded quickly, she gestured to him for his number.

"Forty-two," he whipped back at her.

"Wow, forty-two! Okay, that sounds about right since you're in the military. What are some of your favorite places?"

"Cape Town. That city is amazing, the food is delicious, the people are friendly. It's quite modern. I was pleasantly surprised."

"I have yet to go to Africa. But that's good to know about Cape Town. I'll have to keep that in mind while thinking of new places."

"What's been your favorite?"

"Hong Kong! I had so much fun there. I was even able to navigate the trains with ease. I'd live there if I could."

"Say, it's still early, more vendors will be out in about an hour."

"Really? It seems pretty packed out here already."

"This? No, this is empty. Not even half full," he said then gestured to the iron railings on the Pontalba Buildings surrounding the square. Lisa took pictures of the mule-drawn carriages that were lined up on the road, ready to take people around the French Quarter.

"I like this place, there's so much history here. Do you see those letters in the French Lace?"

"Oh yeah, those are letters. Is that a P?" Lisa squinted at the railings two stories above.

"Yep, AP for Almonester Pontalba. Those are the initials for the woman who helped commission and design this square. She spent a good chunk of her life embarking on a beautification campaign for this plaza. It was a muddy military area before her investment. Her name was Baroness Pontalba. Her father was the wealthiest man in the colony, but he died when she was two years old, making her the wealthiest person in the colony at two years old."

"Wish I had that problem," Lisa commented.

"Yeah, same here," Mike responded. "When she turned sixteen, she was married off to her cousin, the son of Baron Pontabla in France. But he was abusive, and she asked for a divorce after a few years of being in France. Out of anger and hopes to claim the wealth she had inherited, her father-in-law unloaded two dueling pistols into her before killing himself. But miraculously, she survived and went back to New Orleans where she lived the rest of her life with her wealth and title as a baroness. Because with her father-in-law's suicide, her husband became baron and she became baroness. Which gave her the nickname the Bulletproof Baroness."

"That is probably one of the most incredible stories I think I have ever heard. I can't believe he shot her!" Lisa said, shocked and amazed.

"Yeah, it's one of my favorites as well. New Orleans has a lot of interesting characters that have lived here with crazy survival stories like that," Mike said while they slowly walked toward the French Market.

Across the street from the mule-drawn carriages, they encountered a massive line of people, it looked like a club in Hollywood. But it was just the line of tourists waiting to get beignets at Café Du Monde.

"Were you able to try a beignet from Café Du Monde yet?" Mike asked.

"Yes, my family took me here the first night after Muses. We went at midnight, so there wasn't a line."

"Okay, good. I'm glad they did that. So, now we won't have to wait for an hour for you to try one," Mike said in a relieved tone.

"Are you saying you wouldn't want to wait an hour for me?" she joked.

He smiled. "Of course I would. I'd wait all day."

"Really? I wouldn't wait for me," she flirtingly responded. "My uncle mentioned they would have a super long line during the day. He's a secret genius that one. Besides, there's no way I'd wait in that line. I don't have the patience for that wait, and I don't need the calories that badly."

They arrived at a light yellow French designed building. A giant Mardi Gras mask was perched atop the arched entryway under a large sign that read "French Market." The building was long and narrow with one long aisle stretching to the very end. The building was open like one giant metal carport. The food stalls and shops had cages that were able to be pulled down at night. There were ceiling fans and misters to combat the harsh and humid summer months. Fresh fruit stands and food stalls surrounded them. They sold everything from po' boy sandwiches to crepes. A crawfish and oyster bar took up a large part of real estate in the food section. There were tables and chairs for patrons to sit and enjoy the food choices. Toward the end of the market were trinket stalls selling everything from house decor, clothing, and Mardi Gras masks.

"This place makes the best Bloody Marys," Mike said to Lisa as they walked toward the counter of a drink stall named *Organic Banana.*

"That's a bold statement," Lisa replied.

"Trust me," he responded.

"Awesome, I can't wait to try these," Lisa said as she took a photo of the sign.

"Morning," Mike said to the woman working at the counter.

"Good morning. What would you like?"

"Two Bloody Marys please, give it a little lagniappe."

"You got it, that will be ten dollars," the woman said while entering the order into the register.

Mike handed her a $10 bill. Lisa was snapping away at the market, taking pictures of chairs, signs, alligator hides, and the jazz band that was setting up to play. The pickled green beans, olives, limes, and small pickles were displayed in easy reach. The bartender grabbed extra of each to satisfy Mike's request.

"Here you go, sir," the woman at the counter said while she handed him the drinks.

"Thank you," Mike said as he took the drinks and turned toward Lisa, handing her the drink.

"Thanks, it looks delicious," Lisa said as she examined the Bloody Mary.

"You're welcome, let's go over there," he said as he motioned to a park adjacent to the market.

As they stepped down a few steps, they entered Latrobe Park. The park was small and narrow made of mostly cement, with trees and plants outlining the perimeter, it had benches lining the side with a fountain in the middle. Lisa liked how the branches of the trees provided a canopy of shade that covered the benches. It was a quiet place of solace next to the bustling French Market. Lisa followed Mike's lead to a bench next to the fountain. Mike sat down slowly, he grunted like an old man.

"Long night?" Lisa asked, amused.

"Yeah, I think this weekend has officially taken its toll on my body," he responded before taking a sip of his drink.

"Where did you guys go last night?"

"We went out to Frenchman," he said causally. He took out the toothpick and ate an olive.

"What's that? Is that a bar?" Lisa asked curiously.

"It's this street at the edge of the French Quarter. It's where a lot of the music venues are. Moose has a friend whose band was playing at a bar out there, so we went out to support him."

"Were they any good?" Lisa asked while eating a picked green bean.

"Yeah, they were super good. At first, they mainly played covers, which was fine. But then they started to get into their own material, and I was indeed impressed with their style. They had some really good lyrics."

"Cool, what kind of music?"

"Hard to say. I guess I would describe them as if Red Hot Chili Peppers were Cajun, that's probably what I'd say they sounded like."

"I love the Chili Peppers. What's the band called?"

"Can't remember, let me check the Instagram," Mike said as he got out his phone to look at Instagram. "Sawyer, that's what they're called."

"That's an easy enough name to remember. I'll have to check them out. What was that word that you said while ordering the drinks? Lanyard?" Her heart raced as his smile grew. She adored his smile and admired his calm yet strong physique as he sat next to her. She felt safe with him.

"Ha-ha lanyard, naw, lagniappe. It's a local word, meaning give it a little something extra, like extra beans or whatever they choose.

And she sure delivered," Mike said, pointing out the large assortment of vegetables in his drink. "Knowing some of the local colloquialisms helps with getting lagniappe for everything. It sends the message that even though I'm not from here, I know what's up and don't try to get cheap on me."

"Cool, I'll have to remember that one, lagniappe, lagniappe, lagniappe," Lisa said repeatedly to try and remember. "Mardi Gras is exhausting. You almost need to train for it," Lisa said while eating an olive. She lifted her camera to take a picture of the fountain.

"Well, you know what they say, Mardi Gras is a marathon. I'd say I'm getting too old for this, but there were plenty of people out last night way older than me that were outdrinking me. I need to keep it up."

"Yeah, my uncle John is in his midforties and has more energy than I ever will. Next time, this trip won't be on a whim, I'll do proper planning of my liver next year."

"Mardi Gras on a whim, huh?"

"Yeah, I just wanted a quick getaway," Lisa said as she looked down at her feet, she didn't want to get into details of the circumstances of why she wanted to get away. She hoped to keep the day light and free of her drama. "I for sure need to practice drinking more before I come here again. I didn't realize how long it's been since I was in college and could handle this stuff. It's like food. I was really into volleyball when I was younger. Before games, my friends and I would take those graham-cracker sticks and dip them into funfetti cake frosting and just go to town eating a whole box. We'd eat them before nearly every game and still be fine after playing an intense fast-paced volleyball match. But now, if I even have a single piece of chocolate before I go to the gym, I feel like I will throw up."

"Yeah, I know what you mean. That's like when I play soccer. I'll see a guy coming with the ball and I'll think I'm faster than I really am. I'll charge after him, but if I don't do some intentional stretching, I won't last long before something starts to hurt. When I was younger, we'd take shots then go and play a game then be fine to keep drinking after at a pub. But now, I'm out and drinking and barely coordinated to climb on the stairs at my house. I'm amazed I didn't fall on my face last night during Bacchus."

"Ha-ha, yep, and here we are drinking Bloody Marys before noon," Lisa said, holding up her drink as if she was giving a toast.

"This has an ample supply of vegetables and healthy stuff. I think it is perfectly acceptable to drink at any time of day. These are probably the most vegetables I'll eat this entire weekend," Mike said, holding up the drink to his face like a promo model. They both laughed at their terrible attempts at imitating promo models.

"You mentioned you're from Seattle? How long have you been here for?"

"Two years for law school. Before that, I was doing my thing with the Air Force, moving to where they wanted me. When I was twenty-two, I finished college in Boston, then I joined the Air Force and went to Germany and Afghanistan," Mike shared.

Afghanistan, she knew what that meant, he had seen the war face-to-face. She knew not to ask any more about Afghanistan unless he offered. Her father served in the Air Force for thirty years. She grew up knowing how to navigate the return from war questions. And since she barely knew Mike, she didn't want to pry or tap into tough topics, she decided to ask about Boston, a place she had visited. "Boston, huh, what school?"

"MIT."

*He's cute and super smart. Okay, good to know,* she thought. "Boston is a cool town. I went there to visit a friend who was going to BU. We went in the fall. It was so beautiful, the leaves on the trees had turned to the crisp orange. I had always wanted to see the famous New England fall foliage, and luckily, it was everything I'd hope to experience since we don't get such beautiful foliage in Southern California. But what is with the T system? We couldn't catch a train or a cab after 12:00 AM, and we didn't want to pay $200 for an Uber. We walked halfway to my friend's apartment in Cambridge before a cab driver took pity on us. We gave him all the cash we had to take us home."

"Ha-ha, yep! You really had the true Boston experience now. Every local has a T fail story."

"But good cannoli though, my friend took us to this place in little Italy, Mike's Pastry or something," she said, closing her eyes in sweet remembrance. "I will go back to Boston just for that cannoli."

"Ahh, yes, Mike's! You have me missing Boston now. Well, not exactly now. It's way too cold there right now. I'd much rather be out here where there is no snow, and I don't have to wear gloves and can enjoy a cold beverage outdoors," Mike said before taking a bite of celery. "I don't really have any traditions or things I collect. I tried to collect mugs, but they either break or just create unnecessary baggage each time I move," Mike said while looking at the fountain.

"Yeah, I know what you mean. Honestly, for a woman, I don't have that many things. I've moved too much in my life, and I do like the idea of minimalism. Apart from my street art pieces, I don't generally like to have a lot of things in my apartment. I hate clutter, and I like for pieces to have a backstory. I like it for people to come to my apartment and ask where I got something from and what's the story behind it," Lisa said.

Mike nodded. "I'll take you to some great places to get pictures. So, shall we?"

"Let's go," Lisa obliged.

They both stood up. They were awake and energized to take on the day. They walked back inside the French Market, the jazz band was playing loud and with heart.

"All right, let's give you a real tour of the city," Mike said.

As they walked through the French Market, Lisa continued to take pictures of everything. Mainly the menu signs. She spotted one sign that read *alligator, red beans, jambalaya,* she promptly took a picture of it.

"That has to be the most New Orleans sign I've ever seen," she commented.

"Ha-ha, pay attention to the real estate signs. Those are truly entertaining," Mike replied. "Wanna try some gator jerky?" Mike asked Lisa.

"Not really, but okay," she said, giving in. "I might as well since I'm here. When in NOLA, do as the Cajuns do."

"That's why they call this the City of Yes," Mike said. Mike grabbed some samples from the kiosk and handed one to Lisa. She put the sample in her mouth.

She chewed and tried to taste the flavors to decipher the taste of gator meat. "Tastes like chicken," she said while chewing her piece. "Hey, look, masks!" Lisa said while walking toward the masquerade mask section. "The masks are probably one of my favorite parts of Mardi Gras. They're fun and intricately detailed," she said while she was taking pictures of them.

Mike grabbed a bright pink one and held it onto his face. She took a picture of him wearing the mask. "Very handsome," she said. He put the mask back to its spot on the rack. He picked up a floppy blue velvet newsboy combined with a chef's hat and put it on.

"How do you like this one?" Mike asked, sporting a big grin.

"You look fabulous! You know, I'm sure we could get you on a quick flight to Florida. With that outfit, you can totally get to the second round of an audition at a strip mall, and become a member of the next top boy band," Lisa said, her comedic timing never missing a beat.

"Oh man, that's rich! I could take my bedazzler to this and head out to your area in LA to pitch my *Great British Bake Off* inspired show called Drag Chef," Mike said.

"I'd watch it," Lisa replied. "So, you have a bedazzler?" she asked as if she was instigating and teasing at the same time.

"No," Mike said quickly and in a telling tone that implied that he did have a bedazzler. He put the blue velvet hat back on a hook.

"What the heck is this?" Lisa asked as she put a wolf man mask on her face. "What's Rougarou?" Her brow furled as she read the tag that was on the mask.

"It's the Cajun bigfoot," Mike responded.

"Of course, they'd have a bigfoot legend here," Lisa said while taking off the mask.

"Yeah, but it's also used as sort of a way to describe a bad guy or someone who is not to be trusted. Say you date a jerk, your friends would say he acted like a Rougarou."

Lisa thought for a moment. She'd experienced enough jerks, and her ex-fiancé topped the list. She looked at him seriously yet playfully. "Would someone describe you as a Rougarou?"

"Probably, everyone has their moments. But I try my best not to be. Here, this way," Mike said as he motioned toward the back exit of the French Market.

Lisa put the Rougarou mask back on its post and followed Mike. As they exited the market, a bright gold statue shined in front of them. The way the light danced on the gold, it looked like the horse she was on was moving. The base of the statue read "Joan of Arc."

# CHAPTER 15

## *The Maid of Orleans*

THE GOLD ARMOR shined bright and glowed like a fire. Lisa was drawn to the statue of Joan of Arc unlike any statue she had seen before.

"The statue of the lady Joan of Arc was a gift from the people of France to the people of New Orleans. It used to be somewhere over there toward Canal Street," Mike said as he pointed in the direction of Canal Street, "but it was moved due to flooding or something."

"She's beautiful," Lisa said. She felt hypnotized and took more pictures of the gold statue. She walked around it, trying to get the best angle.

"Mardi Gras actually kicks off on January 6th, the day of Epiphany. The Krewe of Joan of Arc is one of the first parades that rolls around the French Quarter on that day. Everyone dresses up in medieval garb."

"It's such an amazing story. She was born a peasant, died a terrible death as a prisoner, then ultimately became one of the most famous women in history. Now her legend lives on centuries later. It makes me wonder if myself or someone I know will become legendary like her. But you know, hopefully for a good reason like her, not for a nefarious reason."

"Bad at the time? Or bad in general like a murderer?" Mike said, "Because at the time, she was imprisoned and executed, she was a criminal."

"That's true. But then again, how do you know what side of history you are on really? During Nazi Germany, millions of people thought they were right and doing a good thing. They believed the propaganda and all the rhetoric. But clearly that was quickly changed."

"Very true. I just try to stay true to my values. I'm pretty sure thou shalt not kill is a pretty universal qualification for being a decent person. I hope that law doesn't change over centuries," Mike said.

"Yeah, hopefully that one won't change," she said as she continued to admire the statue of strength and resilience. Two qualities she desperately hoped to possess.

"Hey, look! What's happening over there?" Lisa said while pointing to a small band playing on a street corner.

Lisa and Mike crossed the street to where the musicians were playing. They stopped to watch and listen to the band. The band members looked young, around high school age. One had a bass, one had a djembe, one was playing the saxophone, and one was playing the keyboard. They were playing the classic New Orleans song, "They All Ask'd for You." Lisa immediately loved the song and started dancing to it. She and Mike danced along with a small crowd of other spectators. After a few minutes of dancing, Lisa turned to Mike and said, "Let's keep moving." Mike obliged and followed her. Lisa put a couple bucks into their tip hat before they walked through a short alleyway toward the river.

A cold breeze greeted them as they found themselves standing on the river bank. Lisa took a deep yoga breath, she loved how lasting and impactful a deep yoga breath was, and how it forced her to take a moment to pause. She felt peaceful and content as she took in the surroundings of the river. The water was choppy and glistened in the sunlight. There was a walking trail as far as she could see in both directions. She wondered if it ran the entire length of the river. Mike walked slowly ahead of her. She walked quickly to catch up to him. As they walked in silence for a few minutes, Lisa reflected on how drastically things had changed in two days. This time last week, she was sitting alone on a beach in California trying to figure out what it meant to find a new normal. Now she was walking along the Mississippi with a new crush, enjoying one of the biggest parties on earth. They walked along the bank toward a waterfront park where a huge stage and dozens of vendors were set up. Locals brought their lawn chairs and set up camp to spend the day watching the concerts and picnicking. A jazz band was playing on stage that had a large black banner across the top that read KING ZULU STAGE in bold gold lettering. A man was dancing around and waving to the crowd, he was dressed in an extravagant outfit of white and gold. The white feathers pointed up in the air high above his head and surrounded him like a peacock showing its feathers.

"I'm assuming that's King Zulu?" Lisa said as she pointed to the man in the feathers.

"I believe so," he responded. "It looks like a few members of an Indian tribe are up there with him too."

"What do you mean?"

"See those group of guys in the bright red feathered outfits and massive head dresses?"

"Yeah, they're hard to miss."

"People that dress in elaborate outfits like that are actually members of the Native American tribes here."

"Oh, wow I had no idea."

"Yeah, their krewes are actually the most secretive. They never post or announce where they will parade. The tribes here are special because they are a mix of the Native Americans and the slaves. When they would escape the plantations, a lot of them would integrate into a local tribe. They're truly their own culture. It's amazing to see the different tribes when they come together. It's a massive rainbow of feathers. The coolest part is that the costumes are all handmade."

Lisa held up her camera to take a picture, she zoomed in on the costumes. She was in awe of the intricate detail of the handmade beadwork. It rivaled the exquisite work of an atelier shop in Paris.

"Sounds like quite the experience. I'll have to keep a look out for them."

Lisa and Mike walked slowly along the bank of the Mississippi River, taking in the glistening river to the left and the sparkling city of skyscrapers to the right, with the soundtrack to the day playing in the background. Lisa took one picture of the river but stopped when she realized that no lens or filter could capture the true beauty of that day. She felt an immense sense of clarity among the chaos the entire weekend represented. There was a gust of wind, enough to make Lisa's hair move and Mike to wince from the chill in the air.

"This is a big runner's trail," Mike said to break the silence of the moment.

"Oh yeah, where are they all now?"

"Hungover probably." Mike laughed. "I get up early and go running out here occasionally with my dog."

"Getting up early and running. Two things in one sentence that I do not do. What kind of dog do you have?"

"Belgian Malinois. His name is Ulysses. He's a veteran too. When I was deployed, my convoy hit an IED, and the hummer I was in flipped. Everyone lived, thank God. But some of the shrapnel got lodged into my arm. I also couldn't hear for a couple days. But when I came back to the states to recover, I had bad PTSD. I found an organization that helps find homes for the bomb dogs and pairs them with veterans. That organization paired him up with me and has been a tremendous help with my PTSD. I feel like we help each other. Though sometimes I feel like he helps me the most."

"I love that he's named after King Odysseus and most importantly another soldier. Plus, I had to read Ulysses in college. I'm not sure if it's genuine love or Stockholm syndrome, but I do love the story of *The Odyssey*."

"Yeah, I had to read it too. Well, I didn't actually read it. I sort of got the cliff notes and sweet talked my way into borrowing notes."

"Ha, is that the only class you did that in?"

"Not entirely."

"Things tend to work out for you, huh?"

"Then, yeah. Now," he shrugged, "not as much."

"Yeah, same here," Lisa said with a laugh. "A war dog? What sort of things does he do? I've seen dogs that are rescued, and it breaks my heart to see their traumas and reactions. What are some of his reactions?"

"At first, he would get scared when riding in a car or going closely to cars he wasn't familiar with. He likes to stick close to me in public, which is good for when I go on walks with him or run with him along this bank. Loud noises still scare him. He preferred to sleep under my bed instead of on a couch or on my bed with me. I was like that too, except for the sleeping under the bed part. But he's getting better. He gives me this sense of comfort that makes me feel better too. It's like we understand each other's pain. I'm sure we would have similar stories and experiences if we could talk to each other. I love him, he's my boy."

Lisa was a dog lover, so it warmed her heart to hear him be so compassionate to an animal that had deep wounds and traumas. She felt more respect for Mike after he shared his story, she also felt more attraction toward him. The band started playing a slower jazz song.

Mike stopped walking. Lisa stopped to see if there was something wrong. He was staring at her with a grin and glow in his eyes, the way every woman wants to be stared at by the guy that she likes. "May I have this dance?" Mike asked as he held out his hand to her, just as he did during the Endymion ball.

"You may," Lisa obliged and took his hand. She immediately looked over his shoulder so he couldn't see her blush; she felt happy, safe, and wanted. It was a romantic moment of just the two of them walking along the bank of the Mississippi River, so close to the city and crowds at King Zulu stage, but yet far enough to feel like they were the only ones that existed.

The song ended, and they kept walking along the bank of the river toward the stage. Within a few minutes, they had arrived in the crowd and were officially in front of King Zulu stage. The band started to play "Tutti Frutti," everyone was on their feet dancing and having fun. King Zulu and the band got off the stage and started a second line. The king's feathers on his regalia moved as if he would be able to take off flying at any moment. The crowd danced and joined in on the second line. Lisa and Mike had arrived to the stage and joined in the second line; they danced and held hands as Mike twirled her. Lisa's cheeks started to hurt from all the smiling. She felt like a kid twirling around without a care in the world.

When the song ended, the band went to the side of the stage for a break. A DJ took the stage and said over the mic, "Don't sit down, y'all, you're gonna wanna dance to this one." Just then, the song "Wobble" started playing from the speakers. Everyone assumed position to do the wobble dance.

"Oh, I know this one!" Lisa said excitedly as she assumed position.

"Good! I'm glad they wobble in California," Mike said as he stood next to her in their line.

They started to dance the wobble in line with the nearly 200 other people at the festival, it was the largest crowd Lisa had ever done a line dance in before. When the dance ended, everyone cheered. Mike leaned over to Lisa and said, "Lundi Gras is a very important day. I love that it doesn't shy away from the Native American and African influence in the city. It feels as if tries to make amends with it by embracing the African and Native American cultures by having it become ingrained into Mardi Gras. Also, it is probably the biggest moneymaker of the season. These tents are local eateries and shops," Mike said as he pointed out the perimeter of the tents and food vendors. "I read in an article about the economics of Mardi Gras, and this one day brings in about five million dollars in revenue."

"Wow, that's really cool. I like that as well," Lisa said loudly as the DJ began playing the next song, which was a Big Freedia bounce song.

The time was now 12:00 PM, Lisa was taking pictures of the stage. Mike turned to her an asked, "How much longer do you have until you need to leave?"

"I have a shuttle scheduled to pick me up at 4:30 PM."

"Okay, let's keep moving on, there's a lot more to show you," Mike said.

The crowd got thicker. Mike grabbed Lisa's hand to guide her through the crowd. Lisa's heart began pounding. She hoped he wouldn't turn around and see her blushing. His hands were rough but not calloused. They were rough enough to indicate to Lisa that she was with a man who knows how to work hard. But soft enough to indicate that he can take care of himself. He was strong, protective, and caring. He was older and experienced. From what she knew about him so far, he had a lot of characteristics she had always looked for in a man. She was excited to be seen, and that he clearly had found her interesting. She was to be pursued for once instead of rejected. She knew that she had fallen for him already.

She liked holding his hand. She liked him taking initiative and guiding her and protecting her. She wanted to tell him how perfect she thought he was, and how imperfect she was. But they powered through the crowd and arrived to the streetcar on Bienville Street just before it left.

The streetcar went along the length of Canal Street. People were everywhere. Revelers had already set out chairs and ladders to claim their real estate along the parade route. Lisa continued to take pictures of the people and buildings she saw along the way. She enjoyed the streetcar ride. She liked being able to observe the city from a different vantage point. The streetcar also gave her a much-needed break from all the walking she had been doing that day. She enjoyed the thrill of not knowing what to expect next. Beads hung from the cables and were wedged in the tracks, but they were no match for their streetcar. The streetcar cut through Canal Street neutral ground like a knife, easy yet cautious.

"Do you know why this is called Canal Street?" Mike asked Lisa.

"Nope," she responded quickly as she took a photo.

"Back in the day, there was a big plan to build a canal here."

"Oh right, my aunt mentioned that the other day. Too bad it was never built. I wonder what it would've looked like? I've been to Amsterdam, and the canals are so cute and unique. They didn't smell at all as opposed to what I've heard about Venice."

"Yeah, I've been there, and I've been to Venice too. Venice smells funky, they were built differently, which is why Amsterdam doesn't smell. But I'm sure any canal here would be a lot muddier and most likely filled with crawfish."

"On second thought, it's probably better they never built the canal. It would probably end up all clogged up with beads and garbage. It for sure would've smelled disgusting given what Bourbon Street smells like."

"Bourbon Street is insane. You really need to be careful, not just for the rowdy people, but the stagnant cesspool puddles are dangerous. When I first moved here, there was a guy in our company who was from San Diego, so naturally he wore his flip flops everywhere. He wore them along Bourbon Street and walked straight through a puddle. A few days later, he was hospitalized with a staph infection." Mike chuckled.

"Oh my god! That's crazy!" she said in astonishment. "It's a good thing I'm in sturdy shoes today. The other day, I saw a girl completely wasted, face down in the gutter with her friends trying to pick her up. I wonder if she's dead now or on an antibiotic drip in the hospital."

"God help her," Mike said while shaking his head. "The next stop is ours," Mike said as he motioned to the stop ahead.

"Okay," Lisa said as she started to reorganize her belongings. They got off the streetcar at St. Ann Street, to the left was a giant white art-deco-looking archway. The archway was an entrance to a large park, with large letters that read ARMSTRONG.

"Cool park," Lisa said while staring at the sign.

"That's a very historical place. A lot of festivals happen there including the New Orleans Jazz fest. But it does have some evil history. That's where they would auction off slaves," Mike said somberly.

"Yikes! That sort of reminds me of people, beautiful and unassuming. How can something so pretty hold such a terrible past?"

"It's definitely a shocking contrast. This way," Mike said, motioning in the direction of the French Quarter.

Lisa took a moment to take a picture of the archway; she admired the architecture of what looked like a simple sign. She then turned toward Mike to catch up to him. They walked a block past traditional French Quarter houses, with the old-world architecture and French Quarter green shutters. Some houses were decorated in Mardi Gras colors and beads. Some were left without anything special to decorate for the season. Every building retained the charm and history of the French Quarter. Each house was colorful and looked like they had a secret to tell. Each house was held in comfort by their iron French lace terraces. Lisa admired the houses and took pictures as they walked along the neighborhood. She came across a real estate sign that made her smile immediately.

"Okay, now I see what you meant about the real estate signs," Lisa hollered as she read the sign aloud, "For Sale, Parking Garage Included, NOT HAUNTED. I love how they have to indicate in capital bold lettering 'not haunted.' You're right, that indeed is the quintessential New Orleans sign I've seen."

He smiled. "Yes! I'm glad you were able to see one in person. Haunted houses are a real concern to real estate prices."

They continued walking until they arrived to Bourbon Street. To the right was a barricade to block the street from cars entering the sea of people at the heart of the Bourbon crowd. To the left were a few other bars and residences and was safe for cars to drive through so that people could get to their houses. Lisa followed Mike as he walked toward a small gray building. The building looked too old to possibly function, but it had decorations out for Mardi Gras, and patrons hanging out on the front porch.

"This is one of my favorite bars, it's called Lafitte's Blacksmith Shop," Mike said as he continued to walk toward the building. The outside was bright, but the inside was so dim she couldn't see past the entryway. Lisa followed Mike into the dark room and felt like she had been transported back to another time.

# CHAPTER 16

## *Lafitte's*

ONCE LISA'S EYES adjusted to the dark room, she was pleasantly surprised at the surroundings she found herself in. The bar was dark and cold, it felt like a haunted house. But with the smiling patrons and staff, everyone was welcome and treated like family. The bar was not crowded or crazy like the other bars on Bourbon Street, it was calm and laid back. A giant fireplace stood in between the bar and the main room with tables. A small fire was lit to provide warmth during the February day. A piano sat silently in the back half of the area that was clear of tables and meant for dancing. Candles shined atop the wooden tables. There were old photographs that lined the walls of the building of New Orleans and paintings of pirates. Lisa followed Mike's lead and walked in the direction of the bar.

"Hey, Mike!" the bartender said as Lisa and Mike approached the bar. The sleeves of his flannel shirt were rolled up as he washed a pint glass.

"Hey, Russ," Mike responded. Russ dried off his hands with a towel in preparation to shake Mike's hand. He threw the towel over his shoulder. "Russ, this is Lisa. She's visiting us from California. She came out for Mardi Gras," Mike said while motioning to Lisa. Mike shook Russ's hand before taking a seat at a barstool.

"Nice to meet you," Russ said as he smiled and extended his hand to shake Lisa's.

She shook his hand. "Nice to meet you as well. This place is amazing," she said as she looked around the bar, taking in her surroundings while swiveling on the bar stool. "What's the story behind it?"

"Well, ma'am, you are about to have a drink at the oldest bar in America. What'll it be?"

"Abita," Mike said.

"Someone recommended I try a very specific drink that's unique to here, but I can't remember what it was," Lisa said as she looked to the side, trying to recall the drink Marcus had told her to order.

"Voodoo Blend?" Russ said.

"No something else."

"Who recommended it?" Mike asked.

"The concierge at my hotel. Obituary! That was it! He said I needed to try an Obituary."

"Ah yes, an Obituary. Coming right up," Russ said.

"Wow, is this really the oldest bar?" Lisa asked. "I feel like I hear that in every old town though."

"Yes, ma'am. A lot of stories can be traced to this place. It was named after the privateer Jean Lafitte. Legend has it he used this place as a trading and smuggling post back in the day. An entire season of drunk history can be played out here," Russ said as he poured Mike's beer from the tap. He continued, "So, how do y'all know each other?" Russ asked as he put down Mike's beer.

"We met at the St. Charles Endymion ball. My family comes here every year for Mardi Gras, and I decided to join them this year. My family left this morning, but I don't have to leave until this evening."

"Aww, so you're going to miss Rex and Zulu then?" Russ said in a sad tone.

"What's that?" Lisa asked.

"Rex and Zulu are two super krewes. Rex is sort of the grand finale where the king of carnival comes out on Fat Tuesday."

"Oh dang! Unfortunately, I'll have to miss seeing Rex. But that's just another reason why I need to come back next year for Mardi Gras."

"But still, it's a good day to be around here and walk around experiencing Lundi Gras," he said as he continued to build her drink on the bar.

"Yeah, it's been really cool listening to the bands playing everywhere. The entire city is one giant party. I've never seen or experienced anything like it."

"Okay, ma'am, here is your Obituary," Russ said as he put the green drink down in front of her. It had a single round ice cube, curved lemon peel, and was served in a chilled champagne coupe on a cocktail napkin.

"This looks interesting," Lisa commented. She picked up her glass to take a drink as Russ and Mike watched and waited for a reaction.

"That is delicious! It's very sweet. Now I understand the name because it is potentially deadly. I could drink these all day."

"Yeah, they are dangerous indeed. Cheers!" Russ said as he held up a Coca-Cola can to both Lisa and Mike. They all three said "Cheers" and took another drink of their chosen beverage.

"That's cool though, you two just hit it off and are enjoying the city. I mean last week you didn't even know each other existed. That's the magic of Mardi Gras, it brings people together," Russ said with a smile. He continued, "What part of California do you live in?"

"Southern California, LA area. Orange County if we want to get specific."

"Aww yes, Orange County, Disneyland."

"Correct, I can tell what time it is based on the fireworks every night. I live about fifteen minutes away from Disney. Now I can see why Walt Disney designed most of Disneyland like New Orleans. This place has the magic and the mystery that he wanted try to create."

"I like California, especially San Diego, now that is a fun city. Did you grow up in Orange County?"

"No, I'm from the north, near Yosemite. I moved to Los Angeles for college when I was eighteen and just stayed down south. Where are you from?"

"Here actually. I'm Cajun on both sides of my family. We were all born and raised near Gretna. I went to LSU. Now I live in mid-city."

"That's awesome. How long have you been working here?"

"Oh, man, technically since college. I did the corporate thing for a bit. I was a full-time accountant. But I hated sitting in the gray cube all day, it felt like a cage. Then the market crashed, I got laid off and got my job back here. That's when I realized how much happier I am here. Plus, I handle all the accounting here too, so it's not like my CPA is going unused. What about you? Are you a photographer?" Russ asked while gesturing towered her camera.

"I do photography for fun. I work in tech. But we'll see what happens. More and more, I feel like grad school might be the next step. I'm sort of in a transition mode of life right now." Lisa stared at her Obituary.

She decided to kill this persona of the cool unbothered girl and take the mask off. She decided it was time to be open and share more about herself. She liked Mike, and she wanted him to know why she was single. The house of spirits served as a confessional.

"I split up with my fiancé a few months ago. Which is why I wanted to come to New Orleans. I wanted to get away, and experience something new and make new memories that don't involve him at all." She continued, "So, in this transition, I'm trying to find what I love again, the ex, he broke me. I caught him cheating on me with his coworker. I feel like the past few years with him were a lie. I'm trying to recapture myself to be honest. I have a good job, but I would love to pursue photography full time. My dream job would be to get paid to travel and take pictures."

"That's too bad about what he did to you. At least you didn't marry the asshole. Travel photography sounds awesome. What's stopping you from doing that?" Russ asked.

"I don't know, student loans I guess."

"I hear you," Mike chimed in. "That's the main reason why I joined the Air Force, to pay for school. You know what they say, the only major you acquire in college is debt."

"Yeah, understandable," Russ said, "but if it's a passion, then you should pursue it. You have your whole life to pay off that loan.

160

For real though, go for your passion before you have real things tying you down, like a husband or something."

"Yeah, it's true, once you have a kid, it's not about you anymore," Mike said.

"Say, this place quieted down a bit. Would you like a tour, Lisa?" Russ asked.

"Absolutely!" Lisa responded with excitement. She stood up with her drink in one hand, her camera in the other, her purse hanging cross body. She followed Russ on a tour of Lafitte's Blacksmith Shop.

Russ led Mike and Lisa around the bar like a museum docent lead a group into an extremely rare and priceless exhibit.

"Lafitte's Blacksmith Shop was built between 1722 and 1732 by Nicolas Touze. It is said to be the oldest structure used as a bar in the United States, although that topic is highly debated. Nevertheless, it is a very old and historical building. The slate roofing protected the building from being completely destroyed by two great fires at the turn of the nineteenth century," Russ said as he pointed out old hand-drawn pictures of the building of what it looked like during that time. "Legend says the two brothers, Jean and Pierre Lafitte, used this building as the New Orleans base for their smuggling operation. They were entrepreneurs, sailors, pirates, and heroes of the battle of New Orleans. The brothers helped Andrew Jackson defend New Orleans against the British by supplying weapons, ammo, and men to help win the war of 1812. We have a funny saying about that battle. They say that if Jackson and Lafitte had been defeated during the battle of New Orleans, we'd all be speaking English here!"

"Ha-ha! Oh my gosh, that is hilarious," Lisa said before taking another drink of her Obituary.

"Since the beginning, New Orleans was a city of refugees, sailors, travelers, tradesmen, adventure seekers, and people on a search for meaning and purpose. As you can see, not much has changed on that end. Also, as a city, we love our traditions, so even though this place has caught fire a few times to the point of near destruction, we still use candles on the tables and light the fireplace. We even remained open during Katrina and served as a shelter and first aid station. Jean Lafitte is a legend in Louisiana, you'll see his name all over the state. But the topic of who he really was is constantly debated. So, Lisa, let's see what you think. Was he the rogue gentleman smuggler? Or was he a nasty trifling mob boss killer who liked to maintain power at any cost?"

"Tough call. I'd say the mob boss since my favorite movie is *Goodfellas*," Lisa said as they continued to walk around the bar.

"Interesting," Russ commented. "Well legend has it that an Italian pirate named Vincent Gambi was upset that Jean Lafitte held so much control. One night, he was able to get a group of guys together to agree that they were going to follow him. Soon after, the Italian pirate stood up and waved his pistol in the air and declared that Gambi's men only follow Gambi. Apparently, Jean Lafitte looked Gambi directly in the eye then shot him dead in his tracks."

"Sounds like a complex character."

"Correct! He's the mascot for a lot of schools around here too. The University of New Orleans are the Privateers."

"What's the difference between a pirate and privateer?" Lisa asked.

"A privateer is sort of a legal pirate. Back then during a war, a nation would issue a letter of mark to a contracted robber with an armada, giving them permission to attack the country's enemy. In return, the contractor will be able to keep the booty of the ships they attack. Jean Lafitte was born in the Bordeaux region of France and was in the maritime business shipping goods around. So, he wasn't necessarily raised as a privateer. I assume he just sort of saw the opportunity to make a lot of money. At the time, a lot of Caribbean and Latin American nations were being established. The United States had not entirely asserted itself as much in the Gulf Coast to establish the same law and order seen in the north. It was certainly a time of political change and chaos. He most likely jumped at the opportunity of being a privateer to capitalize on the emerging nations."

"How did he get so established and mainstream in New Orleans?" Lisa asked.

"He used Grand Isle as his headquarters. His ships would drop anchor and moor along the area, which gave easy access to the Caribbean. He also had a place called the temple near where the town of Lafitte is today. The temple was essentially this warehouse, and people would

LOVE AND MARDI GRAS

come and buy goods he had smuggled. He didn't pay customs taxes or anything, which is what made him an outlaw. But he was so popular with the people that he was able to get away with it. Unfortunately, he also did smuggle slaves and became one of the most productive slave smugglers of that time since the international slave trade was outlawed during his prime years. But right when the authorities were about to arrest him, the British approached him to try and recruit him for the battle of New Orleans. He used the letter from the British as leverage, and worked out a deal with the United States government authorities to help and support the states in exchange for a pardon."

"Whoa, he was that well-known?" Lisa asked.

"Oh yeah, everyone knew who he was," Russ responded.

"How did he die?" Lisa asked, fully immersed in the story.

"Well, as part of the deal for the pardon, he needed to leave New Orleans after the battle. Apparently, he left New Orleans and ended up in Lake Charles, which is why there's legends of buried treasure there. After that, he apparently moved on to Galveston Island where he sort of disappeared. If you go to Galveston Island, there's a lot of urban legends about buried treasure as well. There aren't necessarily a lot of hard facts about his personality or character. My favorite story of him is that he and Marie Laveau exchanged gumbo recipes. But his romanticized character of being the roguish rule breaker is very much alive in pop culture."

He continued, "I think he remains popular here because the personality traits we have seen in the legend sort of personifies New Orleans itself. It's colorful yet dark, it's lively, but a lot of death and destruction has happened here and still happens. Us New Orleanians have a rogue essence to us much like a pirate does, and we like to have a good stiff drink as well."

"Wow, that was such a great tour! I learned so much, thank you, Russ," Lisa said as the tour ended, and they made their way back to the barstools.

Lisa was happy to have received such an intimate tour by someone who was educated and who deeply cared about the subject matter. She would never look at the pirates of the Caribbean the same

163

again. "I have a little over an hour left before I need to head back to my hotel. Any recommendations where I can get some food?"

"Is there anything specific? Po' boy? Crawfish? Oysters?" Russ replied.

"I actually fell in love with the charbroiled oysters last night, and we definitely don't have that in California. I want more of those before I leave," Lisa said.

"Hey, you should take her to the New Orleans Oyster Company then, Mike. It should be open and not too crazy. They have an entrance off Royal Street, so you won't have to walk along Bourbon Street for too long."

"Sounds good, thank you so much, Russ. This place has been a highlight of my trip," Lisa said.

"Of course, darling. Anytime you are in New Orleans, swing by, I'd be happy to see you."

"Most definitely. How much do I owe you, we didn't pay yet," Lisa said as she took her wallet out of her purse.

"I got it," Mike said while pulling out his wallet, "for the tour." He nodded at Russ and put $20 in the tip jar.

Russ gave Mike a friendly smile and a handshake. Lisa gave Russ a hug. The sort of hug you give a good friend, which was how Russ made her feel. Lisa felt like they were kindred spirits. Something inside of her recognized something inside of him. She would surely seek him out the next time she visited New Orleans.

The sunlight burned and blinded Lisa and Mike as soon as they walked outside of Lafitte's Blacksmith Shop.

"Whoa. I did not realize how long we were in that bar," Lisa said while rubbing her eyes.

"Yeah, my eyes are not used to this," Mike responded. They stood blinking their eyes for a few minutes until their eyes adjusted to the light.

"You adjusted?" Mike asked Lisa.

"Yeah, I'm good now," she responded.

"All right, this way," Mike said as they walked down Bourbon Street toward Dumaine Street.

The city was crowded, there were drunk people everywhere throwing beads off balconies to the people below, whether they were asking for them or not. There were street performers and small bands out on the street playing for tips. A man dressed as a Rougarou was taking pictures for tips and doing the thriller dance on a tall wooden box. Frat guys and sorority girls pranced around Bourbon Street in their matching clothes and drinking grenades. Every bar looked like it was a Vegas nightclub with lights, DJs, go-go dancers. People, young and old, were barhopping and drinking out of their go-cups in the street. It was an extraordinary scene that Lisa had never witnessed before.

Lisa grabbed Mike's hand to make sure they didn't get separated as the crowd got thicker and rowdy. They continued onward, pushing through the crowd of people. Lisa felt like she was in a crowded nightclub trying to get through a crowd while everyone was moving in different directions. She could see the sign, Rue du Dumaine. *Just one more block to safety*, she thought. Lisa followed Mike closely. There were only two more bars in between them and the restaurant. When suddenly a small group of women exited one of the bars.

"What the hell, it's Mike Martin," a high-pitched woman's voice said in an ominous tone. She was short, petite, blond, surly, and drunk. She had two other friends with her, but it was evident that she was the queen bee. "Is this your wife? Is this the family that you conveniently didn't mention?"

*Who is she talking to?* Lisa thought. She looked at Mike's face and could see that he was frozen in fear.

"Jen, this is my friend, Lisa," Mike said calmly.

"Oh, your friend," Jen responded with an emphasis on the word "friend." She looked at Lisa and said, "My advice to you, hunny, is to stay away from him. This guy is a damn liar! He only wants to hit it and quit it. He is a piece of shit."

The soberest of her friends quickly pulled her arm to walk in the opposite direction like an angry mother with a toddler throwing a temper tantrum. "You're an asshole!" Jen yelled as she was dragged away from Mike and Lisa.

Mike was unmasked. After a few seconds, he turned and looked at her. Lisa's heart was pounding, but her face remained stoic. She had a look on her face all women give when they witnessed something that took them by surprise, that made them unimpressed and unhappy. She had the Latina look of death that actresses spend hours in front of mirrors trying to learn how to master on cue.

"I'm not married," he said. "I've never been married, just an ex-girlfriend and a daughter."

Lisa was still trying to understand what had happened. All she could respond with was, "Good to know."

"I'll tell you anything and everything."

"Whatever, let's eat," Lisa said. *What the hell just happened?* she thought. *Wife? Daughter? What?* She was shocked and confused at the spectacle. But she didn't want to address it on the street. She needed a moment to download and process what had just happened.

They walked for a few more feet along Dumaine Street then turned right onto Royal Street. They didn't speak to each other, only the sounds of street performers and drunken revelers to accompany their final footsteps to the restaurant. There was no hand holding, no witty or flirty banter, just walking. There was a black sign with white lettering that hung out front that said *Oyster Company*. He opened the door for her, and she walked in.

"Thank you," Lisa said.

She was mad, but she was never rude. She did not look to him as anyone she could hope to be with anymore, she felt like he was a stranger again. She felt that everything she had known and hoped for was a ruse. She quickly recalled all the conversations they'd had over the course of three days. She realized he had never told her anything substantial about his family or upbringing at all. He never mentioned that he had a daughter or even alluded to a daughter. Once again, she fell for a guy before she truly knew anything about him. She had fallen for the idea of him, but not him.

# CHAPTER 17

## Unmasked

"TABLE FOR TWO, please," Lisa said to the hostess as they entered the narrow foyer of the French Quarter restaurant. The restaurant was busy, but there were a few small tables that could fit two people along the front windows.

"Certainly," the hostess said with a smile as she grabbed two menus from the stand, then escorted them to a small table for two.

Mike motioned to Lisa, allowing her walk before him. Lisa felt the beads of sweat along her face. She promptly took her coat off when she got to her seat. She wasn't sure if the restaurant was the reason for her sweating, or if it was the shock and the nervousness knowing they were about to have a serious discussion.

"Your server will be right with you," the hostess said as she handed them menus.

"So, any recommendations?" Lisa said while reading the menu.

"The garlic and bacon one look good. The pizza flavored one looks interesting as well," Mike responded while reading the menu.

"How y'all doing today on this fine Lundi Gras?" the waiter said with a smile as he approached their table. "Can I get you started on any beverages?"

"Bloody Mary, please," Lisa responded.

"I'll take an Abita ale," Mike said.

"Very well, I'll get those right out," the sever said before walking away from the table.

"So, family man," Lisa said, never one to beat around the bush. She put the menu down and looked directly at him. "You never mentioned that you had a daughter once all weekend."

"I thought you just wanted to see the city. It didn't really come up honestly, and was not entirely relevant."

Lisa's heart sank. She thought they were starting to bond. Between the dancing and hand holding, she thought their newfound friendship was more than just a tour guide. She hoped that he was being honest and open with her since he paid her so much attention at the ball and during the parades. But the magic of Mardi Gras was coming to an end, and reality was starting to crash the party. This handsome masked mysterious man of chivalry and mystery. The guy who Lisa held in high regard as being different than the others was in fact, just a regular guy.

"When I was eighteen," he said as he started to tell his story.

"All right, here are your beverages. Bloody Mary for you, ma'am, and an Abita for you, sir," the server interrupted while putting down their drinks and a garlic bread basket. "Now are you ready to order? Or do you still need a few minutes to look over the menu?"

"Yeah, uh, I'll take the parmesan charbroiled," Mike said.

"I'll take the garlic and bacon charbroiled," Lisa said.

"Excellent choices, they'll be right out," the server said as he wrote down the order. He collected their menus and walked toward the kitchen.

Mike tried to share his story again, "When I was eighteen—"

Lisa interrupted, "You know, you don't have to do this. You don't have to tell me anything, it's fine. Whatever. You have a daughter that you never mentioned in the three days we have been around each other. You established your boundaries and clearly have a great sense of privacy around the subject of family and relationships. You wanted that to remain private, I get it. I recognize and I respect the boundary, that's totally okay with me if you don't want to share this."

"No, I want to tell you. I want to be honest with you," Mike said.

"Okay," Lisa said as she shrugged while she picked an olive out of her Bloody Mary and ate it.

"When I was eighteen, I went back home to Seattle for winter break. While I was home, I reconnected with my high school girlfriend. She became pregnant and became angry when I didn't propose or even want to get back together with her. I never truly loved her. I certainly had no intention of marrying her. She's resented me for it ever since. She had our baby, but I have never really been involved in her life. Then when I graduated from MIT, instead of moving back to Seattle, I joined the military. I've always ran from this obligation for some reason. I don't know why." He continued, "Even now, my ex never consults with me regarding important decisions in my daughter's life. I love my little girl. I have never missed a single child support payment. She's on all my military benefits. She's the sole benefactor to my life insurance, 401k, investment accounts. Her medical insurance is through me. I have accounts set up for her education, car, whatever she needs I'm ready for it. Everything I have in my life is hers, and everything I have in my life will be for her."

"But now, the older that she gets, the more I want to be the one to guide her, to teach her things. She's my blood, so I should raise her. But with everything that happened in Afghanistan, with my convoy getting blown to shreds, it's just too difficult for me to handle. Then when I finished my tour and had the choice to end my time in the military or continue once my arm healed, I decided to continue by way of law school. When I told my family about my decision and that I wasn't moving back home, all hell broke out. My ex said some terrible things to me over the phone that I know my daughter probably overheard. I honestly didn't really recognize myself either. I wanted to be the father that my daughter deserved, but I guess I wasn't ready to be that man yet. I took out that confusion with other girls. I hooked up with as many women as I could, hence how I met crazy Jen."

"The girl from outside?"

"Yes, her. Jen was one of the people that took the brunt of my insecurities. Jen was the one I wished I'd stayed away from. She was crazy from the beginning, but she was an easy hook up. She got attached, I got bored and stopped calling. She stalked me on social media and in real life. I considered myself lucky that she was never allowed to get onto the military base. She found out everything about me. She found out that I had a daughter. My ex and I were never married, we were never even engaged. But Jen had somehow convinced herself that I was. Luckily after a few months, she went quiet and just went away. I had always prayed to never run into her. I certainly never wanted to run into her on this day and ruin it. I have been having such a fun time with you. You are an amazing woman, and I suppose I didn't mention my daughter because I didn't want you to think less of me in any way."

"Here you go," the server said while putting the plates of food on the table.

"Thank you," Lisa said to the server.

She felt overwhelmed at the information and the significant part of his life that he seemed to have casually omitted during their time together. She stared at her plate of food then she stood up from the table and said, "Just one second, I need go to the ladies' room."

She needed to be removed from the conversation to truly understand the story he had shared with her. She had just gotten out of a dysfunctional relationship. She felt that she had dodged a bullet with not marrying into a family that had the amounts of issues her ex-fiancé's family had. She did not want to deal with baby mamma drama. She had goals and dreams that she wanted to accomplish. She had a new life to begin. She didn't want to start her new life with any added stress or complications.

While she was washing her hands, she noticed a phrase written on the wall. It read, *When I was older, I used to play with time machines.* "Wow," she said out loud to herself as the words resonated with her.

During the nights of insomnia, she would find herself wondering if she could take a time machine and go back to when she had first started dating her ex, knowing the heartache she felt now, would she do it all over again if she had the opportunity? As painful as her life had been in the past six months, she realized she wouldn't change what she had been going through. Because there's no way the

Lisa of before would be able to recognize the hurt she sees in Mike. She would want to fix him, and in the end, be the one hurt. *Not for me,* she thought and went back out to the table. Mike sat patiently, waiting for her to return to touch his food.

Lisa returned to the table and sat down. She gave Mike a friendly, cordial smile, grabbed the fork and impaled the oyster, put the oyster on a slice of bread, and ate it. *So good,* she thought. The bacon added the perfect flavor and crisp, the olive oil was light and provided the right amount of flavor to enhance the herbs and spices. It was the best oyster she ate the entire trip.

"How do you like it?" Mike asked.

"Delicious."

Lisa felt unsure of what else to say. She felt foolish to have fallen so hard for a man that she had just met. "Do you have a picture of your daughter?" Lisa asked before taking a bite of another oyster.

"Yes, ma'am, I do," Mike said as he pulled his phone out from his pocket and showed her pictures. "She's twelve, she's going to be absolutely beautiful too. I got exactly what I deserved with her. It fills me with rage to know that there are guys out there who will try to hurt her when she's older. It's hard knowing she will get her heart trampled on one day."

"Yeah, she's for sure going to get her heart broken. Even by her own friends, she's going to have some tough times in her teenage years," Lisa said before taking a sip of her Bloody Mary. She kept flipping to the right looking at pictures of his daughter, a few pictures of his dog, Ulysses, were also on his phone. *Not for me,* Lisa thought. She wanted a fresh start, and she deserved a fresh start. Any type of future between them was clearly not going to be able to work out, and she was okay with that.

"Don't worry about your ex. Yes, she may be poisoning your daughter just a little bit, but not all is lost. How often do you talk to your daughter?"

"In some way almost every day, FaceTime, or sending a video message. I'm not sure if she sees them though."

"Does she seem excited to talk to you?"

"Oh yeah, she's always excited, and so am I when I get to talk to her."

"Then you're okay, she's your girl. Now, I'm not even trying to pretend I know the pain in your life, I don't. But based on what you've said, you're a survivor and a fighter. It will all work out for sure," Lisa said in earnest.

"I'm sure banking on it," Mike responded.

They finished their food and sat to finish their drinks even though they could take them to go. They enjoyed sitting together and enjoyed each other's company. Mike paid the bill, and they both got up and walked toward the exit.

"Thank you, Happy Mardi Gras!" Lisa said as she passed by their waiter on their way out.

"Thanks, Happy Mardi Gras to you!"

They quickly headed in the direction toward Jackson Square. "Hurry, let's grab that painting quickly and head to your hotel. We can't let you miss that shuttle. They'll be blocking the roads off soon for the parades tonight, and you'll miss your flight," Mike said as they walked quickly, past touchdown Jesus, through a side street, and was spit right onto the square in hopes to buy the painting she saw earlier. They stood and stared around the square, trying to locate the booth they wanted, but there was no sighting of the artist.

"Oh, no he's gone. Man, that sucks," Lisa said in disappointment.

"I'm sorry, it's all my fault we should've came here before the restaurant," Mike said, sympathetic to her upset feelings.

"No, it's all me. I should've bought it while I had it."

"Want me to send you one when he gets back here tomorrow?" Mike asked in a desperate attempt at redemption.

"No, it's okay. I'll be back here one day for sure. I will get one then," Lisa said in a defeated tone.

She looked around Jackson Square, the cathedral was glowing, the sun was shining, the lighting was perfect. It was a light which allowed for everything to be seen clearly. Light rays reflected off the glass windows, creating the feeling of magic, surprise, and discovery. A single saxophone player played the song "You Are My sunshine"; it was the perfect song for the sunny day.

172

She stared at him and smiled. "But you know what?"

He stared back. Sheepishly, he said, "What?"

"I think I found my masterpiece right here," Lisa said as she lifted her camera and zoomed in on Mike's face and took a picture.

It was the only picture she took of him the entire weekend. He was smiling ear to ear and stared into the camera. He had no mask on, no crazy hat, nothing to distract from who he was, it was just him. The white of St. Louis Cathedral was illuminated in the background, with people and trees blurred, everything around him was a little blurry in the photo, except for him, Mike was clear as the saxophone's tuning. Lisa smiled at him, he stared at her the way all women want to be stared at. But the butterflies were gone, she felt peace after learning who the real Mike was. There would be no open ends. She would not return to California thinking about the one that got away; the mystery to him had been solved. In that moment, she realized the source of peace she felt did not come from a man or a relationship. It came from the city. It came from being thrown into a different culture and new experiences, which caused her to open herself up to new things, foods, ideas, and people. She felt alive and rejuvenated. She reconnected with her family, and to who she always was. Her source of happiness came from the city and the spirit inside of her. Which made her happy to have finally realized that.

"Let's get you back to your hotel," Mike said.

"Yes, let's," she obliged and followed him as he led the way out of Jackson Square.

They walked side by side, no holding hands. A small tension remained between them. They knew this day was coming to an end, but they didn't know how to end it.

"What hotel are you staying at?" Mike asked.

"The Roosevelt," Lisa responded.

"Wow, fancy," Mike commented.

"Yeah, not a bad hotel to invite myself to. John and Joan know how to vacation," she responded.

"I still think it's great how you decided to travel last minute," Mike said.

"Me too, this has been a monumental weekend for sure," she replied.

They walked toward the alleyway toward touchdown Jesus, down Royal Street where they got caught up in a second line. The band was playing the song "Iko Iko." Lisa and Mike observed for a quick moment before they realized they didn't have much time before the shuttle would be waiting to take her to the airport. The walkers in the parade were a small krewe of women throwing roses and beads while dressed like 1920s flappers. Lisa and Mike powered through the parade before it turned left onto Conti Street, providing Lisa and Mike to walk in relative peace the rest of the way to Canal Street.

"I like The Roosevelt. They have the best Christmas display in the city. My friends and I always go there during Réveillon," Mike said as they stood in the neutral ground of Canal Street waiting to cross.

"What's Réveillon?" Lisa asked as they started to cross the street, walking toward her hotel.

"It's a type of food festival that happens during the Christmas season. People have all-night dinner parties either at home or at a restaurant. The restaurants and hotels have special menus and tasters that are only allowed to be served during that season. It's actually a pretty organized thing because participants submit their menus to be on the official guide. It's sort of like a restaurant week. One of the things my friends and I do is we will start at one bar to grab a small bite. Then take our go-cups and walk around the quarter and CBD to the different hotels and restaurants to see their Christmas displays, all while eating along the way. We call it Christmas treating instead of trick-or-treating."

"That sounds like so much fun! I think I need to just come here for one year and indulge in every festival and special event this city has to offer," Lisa said.

"That sounds fun but also scary for your liver," Mike responded.

"Ha, very true, that's a lot of drinking," Lisa said as they approached the entrance of the hotel.

"Welcome back, Ms. Perez," the doorman said as he opened the door.

"Thank you, sir," Lisa said as she and Mike walked off the winter streets of New Orleans, into the warm hotel that felt like a cozy house instead of a hotel lobby.

The warmth on her face, combined with the soothing smell of citrus and sage, caused all of Lisa's senses to be reset and calm as she and Mike walked across the marble floors of the hotel lobby. They walked slowly under the radiant chandeliers, alongside the other hotel guests sporting their beads hanging from their necks like Olympic medal winners. As they walked closer to the concierge desk, the mood shifted from calm to somber. They were both trying to hold on to every step they had left with each other. Lisa led the way as she approached the concierge desk. She looked for Marcus, but he was not there. She pulled out her wallet to find the claim ticket for her stowed items.

"Hi, I need to get my bags," Lisa said as she gave her ticket to the woman working at the concierge desk.

"Great," the woman responded with a smile, and she took Lisa's claim ticket then asked, "May I see some ID please, ma'am?"

"Yes, of course," Lisa said as she opened her wallet to get her driver's license.

The woman compared the license to the name on the ticket and the computer screen. "Excellent," the woman said while she confirmed the corresponding information. "Also, your shuttle is here waiting for you, Ms. Perez," the woman said as she handed Lisa back her license. She opened the drawer and grabbed the keys to the storage closet where her bags were stowed, then emerged from the closet with Lisa's luggage.

"Here you go, Ms. Perez. Would you like a bottle of water for the road?"

"No, that's okay. I'll be fine until the airport. I don't want to have to throw a half empty bottle away for the security line."

"Okay, great, well I hope you enjoyed your stay, and we would love to have you back. Have a safe flight home to California, ma'am, and Happy Mardi Gras."

"Thanks, Happy Mardi Gras."

Mike grabbed her bags and carried them for her as they walked in silence toward the golden doors where the shuttle was waiting. The doorman opened the door and with a nod said, "Have a safe flight, Ms. Perez."

She smiled. "Thank you."

The shuttle driver swiftly got out of the van and walked toward Lisa and Mike. "Ms. Perez?" he asked to confirm she was the passenger.

"Yes, that's me," she responded.

Mike smiled and nodded at the driver and handed him Lisa's bags to load them into the trunk. Lisa and Mike stood side by side, they waited on the steps in silence to see who would say goodbye first.

"Orpheum Theater," Lisa said awkwardly, reading out loud the signage across the street from the hotel for the Orpheum Theater that sat dim and vacant. The biggest show in the city would be free on the street later that evening. She didn't know what else to say.

"You're right," Mike said.

Confused, she asked, "About what?"

"Until recently, as in the past few years since Afghanistan, life has been rather easy on me. Being in the military has oddly saved me from myself. I was selfish, inconsiderate, and hated responsibilities. I realize that the military has shaped me into someone I want to be, but I still lack the courage to truly grab the reins and become that person."

"Wow, the fact that you acknowledge any shortfalls and realize you are still not where you want to be is a massive step. I'd say you are on your way." Lisa was still confused and wondered what exactly was going on inside his head.

He turned to face Lisa and said, "I'm sorry I wasn't open with you about my daughter. But I just want to say that I think you are absolutely beautiful. Not just because of your looks, although you are absolutely drop-dead gorgeous. Your beauty transcends the physical, you are beautiful for the way that you think and how kind you are to everyone. For the first time in a very long time, I felt like I was valued by someone. Your smile makes everyone smile. Everywhere you go, you are able to connect with someone, and I admire that so much. I'm sorry to bombard you with this information, but I wanted you to know how I felt, especially since I omitted a very important aspect in my life already. I didn't want to omit how I feel around you. I wish we had more time together, but since we don't, I'd really like to keep in touch."

Lisa looked into his eyes, and she could see the sadness that he held inside of him, he was unmasked, he was open and vulnerable for the first time.

"Wow, thank you for those kind words. Yeah, of course, we'll keep in touch, you have my number, feel free to use it," Lisa said casually as she looked into his eyes. But she didn't feel the warmth, hope, and butterflies that she had felt earlier. She was flattered by what he had said, a part of her had wished he had said it earlier. But a part of her was grateful that he didn't, because it would've made leaving him harder. She didn't expect to keep in touch, she didn't really want to anymore.

She realized that the person she needed to meet in New Orleans was herself. The person she needed in her life was herself. The only person who could complete her, was a complete version of herself. She was excited to go back home and continue to move on. Lisa stared at the ground for a second, then stared up and looked at Mike. She faced him and looked at him directly into his eyes and said, "I see you, Mike."

She gave him a kiss on the cheek and said, "You are a good man. I can tell you have a good heart, but like all of us, our egos get in the way. I know you'll find your path, and when the time is right, you will make the right woman happy."

As she started to walk away toward her shuttle, when she got to the door, she turned around, smiling ear to ear, she made a small waving motion, mouthed the words, "Bye." She climbed into the shuttle and sat down.

As the van drove away, Lisa looked back to get one last look at Mike. She watched Mike as he stood on the steps of The Roosevelt Hotel with his hands in his pockets, head cocked back; he looked defeated. He walked down the small steps onto the curb and headed toward the French Quarter. She turned around, sat forward, and stared at the road ahead.

# CHAPTER 18

# Homecoming

LISA ARRIVED AT the airport and went through the same motions as all airport security lines: coat off, shoes off, purse in a bin, arms up, through the body scanner, then out to regroup and onward to her assigned gate. She could tell exactly who was coming and who was going by if they were wearing beads or not. Rookie revelers that were leaving the city had a look and posture of a walk of shame and pain. They were tired, sick, and worn out. It was a look Lisa saw on her twenty-first birthday she celebrated in college. She sat down at her terminal and stared at her plane that sat at the gate, patiently waiting for new passengers. She felt a buzz in her pocket from her phone. Lisa's heart skipped a beat. *Mike?* Lisa thought, but was not as excited as she had been earlier when he texted. She took the phone out of her pocket. She looked at the screen, it was Allison checking in on her.

ALLISON: Hey, girl! Are you at the airport yet? How's the guy?
LISA: Hey! Yes, I'm bored at the airport just sitting at my gate. The guy was a bit of a flop. The more I got to know him, the less I liked him. It was a fun day exploring the city with him. But anything else, no way. You need to come with me to Mardi Gras next year! You'd love it here.

ALLISON: At least you don't have to see the guy again. Actually, I took a look at your chart, and Friday night held great energy for you in terms of intuition and manifestation. So, either way, exploring the city was a good thing for your journey. And yes! I for sure want to come with you next time.

LISA: Well, manifestation definitely occurred. I feel like a new person, and I'm actually excited to come home.

ALLISON: Great! I can't wait to hear more when you get back. Have a safe flight. Xoxo. Love and Light!

LISA: Xoxo. Love and light!

Lisa put her phone back in her pocket. She turned on her camera and looked at the pictures she took throughout the day. Pictures of the French lace, beads stuck on lampposts, masks, art, the Mississippi River, people dancing, ladders posted waiting to be filled with their kids, families celebrating happily together, the French architecture, the statues on the streets, the manhole covers, and Mike. His smile, his face, he looked handsome frozen in time in the snapshot she got of him in Jackson Square. She could see the hurt in his eyes but ambition shown in his smile. He was surrounded by the blurred background, but the light from the cathedral seemed to protect him. She would for sure get it printed and save it. She didn't know why she wanted to print it, it was one of the best candid photos she'd ever taken, she felt she needed to have a hard copy so it wouldn't be accidently deleted.

"Group B, we are now boarding group B," the gate attendant announced over the intercom.

Lisa stood in response to her boarding group being called. She felt relieved to be heading home. She also felt a sense of irony. In the span of three days, as excited as she was to leave Los Angeles, she was surprisingly excited to go back.

As her plane took off, she sat in her window seat and stared at the city below. The sky was dark, the Superdome was illuminated in purple, green, and gold. She could see boats on the river, and the Central Business District buildings below sparkled radiantly as if they were celebrating Mardi Gras as well. She tried to look and see if she could see any parades rolling, but the plane turned and switched directions, and all she could see was the night sky. *Well damn,* she thought, fully acknowledging that the small chance of a new romance that weekend was gone. Lisa wondered what Mike was doing, and as true to her perfectionist nature, she recounted every moment of the day they spent together. She stared out of the window into the night sky, thinking of what she would've said and how she would say it. She thought about ideas for what she would do differently and how she would've approached Mike had he been open with her at the beginning about his daughter. She thought about the food, her family, and their faces. She also pondered New Orleans, the City of Yes. She wondered if there was perhaps more meaning behind the nickname.

She reflected about the morning she left Los Angeles and what she was hoping to accomplish during her quick trip to New Orleans. She thought about how foolish she felt by wanting to find a guy to rebound with and take her mind off her ex. But she realized that she was more successful during this trip than she had originally intended. She had indeed been able to recapture the happiness that she longed for when she left Los Angeles.

In that moment on the plane, she realized that she wasn't going back to California without finding love. She found a love that was more important than the love of a new boyfriend. She found a new love that she did not expect to encounter three days ago when she flew to New Orleans; she fell in love with New Orleans itself. She fell in love with the people's resilience. She fell in love with the architecture. She fell in love with the culture. She fell in love with the food. She fell in love with the magic of Mardi Gras, which surprised her and captured her heart the most. She knew she'd join her family's tradition and come back year after year to deepen her newfound love. She found the missing piece that she felt was missing from her life.

She found the person that she needed to find the most. She found the person she was looking for all along, herself. She felt rejuvenated and excited to officially start her new beginning. Lisa was ready to move forward and carry the City of Yes mentality with her to California.

"You can live in any city in America, but New Orleans is the only city that lives in you."
—Chris Rose

# *Acknowledgments*

THANK YOU TO all who have in some way either knowingly or unknowingly provided support or inspiration to this story. Jim and Tina Peña, with whom introduced me to New Orleans. Brandi Manthei, Debbie Manthei, Heavynn Shy Peña, Romie Newman, Shyra Caligiuri, Jennifer Tripsea with whom I've sat for hours talking, drinking, and tailgating along the Mardi Gras parade routes.

My parents, Sam and JoAnne Peña, Melissa Velasco, Hila Shmilovich, Laura Pulido, Samantha Diele, Ginnie Siverly, Caitlin Williams, Schauna Porter, Arreana Joseph, Jennifer Gomes, Michelle Dixon, Gabe Madrigal, Osanna Bennet, Len Komar, Lisa Hsiao, Lindsay Felchle, Cynthia Colk, Amanda Johnson, Alberti Paz, Alicia Prescod, Natalia Pollock, Kat Koszewski, Maurine Taylor, Emily Dyck, Arianna Caligiuri, David Fernandez, Sara Wilson, whom this book is dedicated to, and all the writers from AlteaArte, Joe Fuentes, Robert Armani, Allison Kluger, Dawnmarie Deshaies, Ling Ling Leoh, Erica Presley, Joe Espinoza, Gina Tucker, Grace Choi, Coral Wilson, Ericka Colombo.

*Laissez les bons temps rouler.*

# About the Author

LAURYN PEÑA HOLDS a bachelor's degree (BA) in English literature and a Master of Business Administration (MBA). She has a passion for traveling the world and experiencing everything life has to offer. She currently resides in Orange County, California. On the weekends, you can find her playing volleyball on the beach of Corona Del Mar or in a yoga studio.

Instagram: @Laurynep